A KENTUCKY COWBOY'S LOVE

BOURBON CREEK ROMANCE 1

DINAH PIKE

Mom,
I dedicate this book to you.
It does my heart good to know that when you made your list of 70+ romance novels to read this year, one of them was written by your daughter, Dinah.
I could not have found a better mom if I had spent a life-time looking. We are all so lucky to have "Granny" in our lives.

CHAPTER 1

*S*avannah Stetson looked out over the bank parking lot from the view she had in front of her teller window. It was a slow, June middle-of-the-week lull before things picked up in the afternoon.

When it was this quiet it was hard not to get sleepy at work.

The quiet was shattered by a big white truck with black fender flares. As it screeched by, Savannah could see the guy in a John Deere cap gunning the engine. Vroom Vroom!

Ugh. Him again. I'm not going to think about YOU! People think I'm like you because I dated you.

After a moment the white truck roared by in the other direction, honking its horn.

Good grief! Go away! I didn't know you were such a rotten little snake.

"For the love of all things country, grow up already," Savannah said aloud.

"Hey. Don't let that excuse for a human get under your skin," said Lana, the girl working the next counter.

Savannah smiled and nodded. Lana was right, of course.

When it was quiet again, her mind wandered, and it wandered to other men.

Maybe I need to be a free spirit these days. I'm going to imagine flirty thoughts about all the men that come in here this afternoon, she thought. *I need someone new to cut up with, someone to take my mind off the past.*

Just then a very frail old gentleman opened the door and shuffled across the lobby to the men's restroom. He was wearing a floral print shirt, golf shorts, and crocs with black socks.

She quickly amended her statement. *Maybe I'll just have flirty thoughts about men that come to my teller window specifically.*

I've got to get out of this town, she said to herself for the thousandth time that summer. *There aren't enough interesting men around, no great jobs, and I'm tired of being "daddy's perfect little girl" on the farm. I'm tired of this small town life.*

I'm tired of being pointed out for my questionable choices. None of that was my fault.

I'm tired of that noisy white truck!

I need some excitement in my life.

Savannah Stetson didn't know it then, but never-to-be-forgotten excitement was about to walk in the door of that bank.

She watched a shiny red Ford F-150 pull into the parking lot and shut off. A very attractive cowboy opened the door and slid down out of the truck like a big bobcat on a ledge with his prey in sight. "Very attractive" didn't begin to cover what she was looking at. "Rugged, solid, male perfection" might come closer.

She hoped he came closer.

Something about the way he moved really caught Savannah's eye. *Wow, now, that's more like it,* she thought to herself as her heart rate kicked up a notch. *Walk toward me, cowboy.*

The guy in dark jeans, faded at the knees, a functional fitness T shirt, and a beige cowboy hat walked toward her like a man on a mission.

She could hardly catch her breath by the time he took off his hat and laid a check on her counter.

"Can I help you? With... anything?" she asked, never breaking eye contact. His eyes were a bright clear blue.

"I'd like to open a checking account and get a debit card. Am I in the right place?"

"You sure are," she said as she wondered why her cheeks were warming up. She guessed it was because he was the kind of man she could hardly keep it together around. She'd much rather just reach over the counter and... literally drag him over it, so that she could get much closer to him. Wouldn't that make heads turn in this place!

She smiled at him and glanced down to see that there was no wedding band. "You new around here? I haven't seen you anywhere - I think I would remember."

"Yeah. Just got hired out at the Stetson place. That's really the name of the ranch - Stetson. Can you believe it?" He smiled, and pointed to his cowboy hat. It was a Stetson.

His smile is full of secrets - secrets and orange blossom honey swirled into a glass of very good bourbon.

"Oh, I can believe it. I live there myself."

"Seriously?" He smiled again and her heart flipped over in her chest.

"Yeah. Small world, huh? So, my daddy hired you on?" Savannah was leaning closer to him while pretending to look at the check. Then she remembered to hand him some paperwork to fill out. "What's your name?"

"Brody. Brody Bangfield."

"Seriously?" she asked as she tossed her hair over one shoulder.

"Yes - that's my name."

Whoa, girl, she thought, *could this get any better?* She sure hoped so, and soon! "That seems like a name that could get a man into all sorts of trouble," she flirted. *Look at the muscles in those arms... I wonder if they are as hard as they look.*

"Well, maybe, but I try not to mix business with pleasure, especially when it comes to my new boss's daughter." He playfully knocked his knuckles on the counter. "What a shame. What's your name...besides Stetson?"

"Savannah," she laughed while batting her eyelashes. *Oh my gosh,* she thought. *I just literally batted my eyelashes at this hunky cowboy while I want to imagine batting my eyelashes along his neck, slowly, while he struggles for control...*

"You ok?" He was staring at her in concern. "I feel like I lost you there for a second."

"Oh! Sorry. My mind wandered. Here's some counter checks to get you started. We'll mail the others to you." She looked down at his address. "Yeah. You're staying at the bunkhouse?"

"For now. See if I like it."

"Oh, Brody Bangfield, I do think you're going to like it." She gave him her best smile.

"Thanks. Maybe I'll see ya around."

"Maybe you will," she said as he walked toward the doors.

I certainly am going to try my best to make that happen. Who could imagine that cowboy would take old Sylvester's place when he finally retired? Thanks, daddy...

"Savannah? Earth to Savannah?" Lana, her best friend since first grade, had tried to hear the whole exchange.

Savannah only turned toward her co-worker when Brody had driven completely out of sight. "What? So, I zoned out for a minute there."

Lana grinned and said, "I saw that."

"Well, weren't you staring, too? Did you see that jawline of his?" Savannah sighed.

"OH, yeah. I also noticed his backside in those jeans as he

walked out the door. You are a lucky girl, since you know his name now."

"Ha. I know where he works, too." Savannah nearly jumped up and down. "Ready? At the ranch! Daddy hired him." She fanned herself dramatically with some money envelopes. "I've got to find ways to run into him! You'll help me, right?"

Lana laughed. "Well, I guess so. It seems like your summer is looking up, Savannah Kay! It sure looked like some chemistry between you two." She clapped her hands together. "See? Just because you've been hurt, you never know when things might turn around. You gotta' promise to share all the DETAILS!"

CHAPTER 2

$\mathcal{B}$rody swung the 55 lb kettlebell overhead for the twenty-first time. He put it down and took off running up the grassy hill.

This ranch sure is a pretty place, he thought as he reached the crest and turned around.

Kentucky is a pretty area of the country. Savannah Stetson is a pretty Kentucky girl, too, while I'm listing pretty things.

There I go thinking about her again!

Stop it.

Focus on the workout.

His breathing deepened as he ran back to the kettle bell. His shoulders, back, and arms pumped out 15 swings without any break in rhythm. He figured he could list 15 attractive things about her during the next hill sprint easily enough, just to keep his mind off of his calves.

Her army-green eyes, shiny reddish blond hair, perfectly tilted eyebrows, the lilt in her voice, her brave and flirty ways, her glossy lips, and a smile that a man would do a lot to see again, her way of looking right into his soul...

Whoa, there, cowboy, that's a little much! I only saw her for maybe ten minutes.

He wondered when he might see her next. He knew he was going to be watching for her all the time.

He commanded his mind to think through a to-do list on the farm. He needed to learn the lay of the land, and the borders. There was a lot of fencing to check and most of it looked solid. Some of what he had seen where the fencing was shared with an elderly lady needed attention first. The daily chores would fall into a rhythm soon enough.

After 9 more swings and the last run up the hill, Brody sank to the grass and looked at the sky while his breathing recovered. He couldn't concentrate on the tasks at hand today. This workout was supposed to clear his head.

Heck, even the clouds here are pretty today. But, not quite as pretty as Savannah Stetson.

As a cooling June breeze blew over him, he shook his head. He tried to get that girl off his mind and headed toward the bunkhouse for a quick shower. Then he was heading out to check as much of the property's fencing as he could before a late lunch with Glenwood Stetson. He hoped there was a solid budget for the needed upgrades.

Brody's new boss seemed like a straight up kind of guy to work for and Kentucky was far enough away from Montana to give some distance to his old life there.

Brody needed to work, to keep busy, and to build a new life. He was tired of always walking away. He wanted to forget his old boring life, where he could not stop comparing himself to his older brother and stayed way too long in the wrong relationships.

CHAPTER 3

Savannah's brain was on automatic at work as she
counted out her drawer to start another day. She sent
up a little prayer of thanks that the amount matched the day
before. She was in the little drive-thru area of the bank so it was
harder to talk to her colleagues.

She was in a good mood and ready to slay the day. Her mind
wandered and she talked to herself, like usual, while the Steve
Miller Band played The Joker. What was a space cowboy,
anyway?

I need to go shopping for new lingerie...wonder if anyone makes a
matching panty and bra set in a bucking bronco print? A certain
cowboy might really appreciate that choice, haha.

I can't believe I even thought about Brody Bangfield while getting
ready for work this morning. I chose my red and white gingham set
with white eyelet trim, but I know HE'S not going to come back into
the bank today, since he was just here a few days ago. Oh, well, it's fun
for me! But, I was definitely thinking too much about that cowboy
while getting ready.

Savannah noticed the bank's canned music was now playing

Rhinestone Cowboy. That was a classic cowboy song if ever there was one.

Oh, I want to kiss that new cowboy.

I'm going to do it, too! And why not? I'm leaving this crazy little town soon enough, so there won't be any baggage or worries or running into him later, or broken promises, or any of that crap that seems to follow me whenever I even LOOK at a man twice!

NO strings, that's my new motto.

What's the worst that could happen? He might push me away. Well, I won't know if I don't try.

The very next background song she noticed was Aerosmith's Back In the Saddle Again.

These songs! Coincidence? Did Lana program cowboy songs somehow this morning?

I thought I would be running into that new cowboy a lot at home by now, but no luck. Yet.

She had worked outside a lot when she would get home from the bank, hoping to run into Brody. She'd ridden her horse, Buttercup, and brushed her until she shone in the afternoon light. She'd pulled weeds. She had washed her own car in the driveway, twice!

She wasn't quite out of ideas though.

I think I'll go home for lunch. I can't kiss him if I don't run into him, right, Savannah? Go for it. Try a new timeframe.

SHE THOUGHT about her last visit to Mizz Myrtle. She had felt a need to tell the sweet old neighbor all about how hurt she had been when her last boyfriend had betrayed her so publicly and how she had been stuck in a sort of painful swirl of wondering who was whispering about it constantly.

Miss Myrtle had said, "Well, girl, you always did worry things to death in your head ever since you were knee high to a goat. You have to square your shoulders and move on. You know who you are."

Savannah had always run to the old farmhouse down the road so she could talk things over with her. She was about to burst with news of how an extremely handsome cowboy had showed up in the bank and suddenly her heart had felt unbroken.

Mizz Myrtle had leaned on her hoe in the garden and reminded her of a few things. She didn't mince words, of course. "Now, don't get too big for your britches. Remember what a sweet girl you are, and act like it. This new fella will see you for who you are, if that's what you show him! Don't scare him off, Miss Savannah."

Savannah knew that Mizz Myrtle's advice had never steered her wrong.

LATER, she went home for lunch. She pulled her little Honda down the drive toward the main barn. Maybe she would see Brody if she thought of a reason to hunt down her dad. That was perfect. She would start with the biggest barn.

Coming quietly into the dark of the barn, she walked down the row of stalls, smelling hay and cows and leather. She stopped as she heard something in the stall right in front of her - someone singing, low and quiet.

"Yippy ti yi yo get along little doggies
it's your misfortune and none of my own
Yippy ti yi yo get along little doggies
you know that Wyoming will be your new home"

SHE SLOWLY LOOKED over the stall door and there sat Brody Bangfield, leaned up against the door and scratching the curly hair on the head of a little brown calf.

He was singing an old cowboy song! His voice was kind of like velvet... so when he stopped singing the chorus, she took a deep breath and started the verse.

"While I was walkin' one mornin' for pleasure
    I spied a young cowboy just ridin' along
    His hat was throwed back and his spurs were a jinglin'
    And as he approached he was singin' this song"

BRODY LOOKED up at her with that crooked smile and slowly stood up and turned straight toward her. His face was inches from hers.

She could not believe how hard her heart was knocking.

She looked up into his eyes and suddenly couldn't for the life of her remember the rest of that song. His blue eyes were mesmerizing, to say the least.

"Now, how does a Kentucky girl know the words to that song?"

"Oh, I had a very fine music teacher in elementary school." She tried to lean even closer to him. "It seems like there's always something between us, Brody Bangfield, like a bank counter... or a stall door."

By this time she was on tip-toes with her hands an inch away from his on the top of that half-door. Was she imagining that he was ever so slowly dropping his head towards her? His eyelashes were incredible, his lips were scant inches away.

She reached up and put her hands on the back of his neck

and just before she kissed him she said, "You sure do sing pretty. Somehow, I'm not surprised."

"I could say the very same thing, but I'd rather do this." He barely got these words out as they both closed their eyes, and connected.

Brody's first kiss with Savannah absolutely took her breath away.

She eventually caught a tiny bit of air, then went back to losing herself in the swirling feelings of his lips on hers, his breath speeding up, his tongue just beginning to dance along her lower lip. Oh!

"Are you coming out or am I coming in, because this door is in the way," Savannah whispered into Brody's neck, hoping that her breath would give him shivers along his spine.

She had finally run into her cowboy and she wanted more kisses.

"Hey! Hey, Savannah? You in there?"

Savannah and Brody instantly pulled apart when they heard Glenwood Stetson enter the barn, his big voice booming out.

Oh my gosh! Dad! What bad timing!

"Hey, dad!" She stepped back toward him and kissed his cheek, hoping her cheeks weren't as flushed as they felt right about now. "I was, um, looking for you, to see if you wanted to have some lunch with me, and, I, well, I heard singing."

By this time Brody had come out of the stall. He reached over and shook Glenwood's hand.

"I was putting this little calf at ease before I took her to the lower pasture where her momma is."

"You sing to the cows?" Glenwood asked.

"Yes, sir, when they need to be calmed."

"I seem to be getting my money's worth with you, son!"

Savannah got her dad's attention again. "Lunch?"

Glenwood turned toward Savannah as he clasped the cowboy's broad shoulder. "No, Brody and I have planned a lunch meeting, little darling. We might just bore you to tears talking about the cost of fencing and rotational grazing patterns. But, you can join us if you want to. We might even have a shot of bourbon. Glad to see you two met."

"We met a few days ago at the bank." they both started to say at the same time, then laughed.

Savannah declined the lunch meeting. "No, I've got to get back to the bank in a few. I'll grab a sandwich. Now, daddy, don't go drinking any Four Roses without me!"

Glenwood chuckled. "We'll keep to the Maker's Mark."

"See you around, Miss Savannah," Brody grinned at her like he couldn't wait to pick up where they had left off.

She practically floated back to her car.

As GLENWOOD WALKED Brody up to the main house for their meeting, he talked about Savannah a little. "That girl of mine - so smart. She is wasting her talents on a little bank teller job."

Brody memorized every detail about Savannah. "What else is she good at?"

Glenwood laughed. "She's good at everything she ever tried to do. Maybe that's part of her problem. I never know what crazy thing she's going to come up with next. Changes her mind every five minutes! Why, last month, she told me had sworn off all men for good!"

They both laughed at that, for very different reasons.

CHAPTER 4

*A*fter lunch, Lana watched Savannah from across the bank lobby. That girl had a little bounce in her step and a smile as big as Mammoth Cave. She hadn't looked that happy in way too long.

Lana knew something was up and couldn't wait to try to get it out of her after work. Savannah would tell her but she had to wait until they could settle in over dinner. The clock sure went slowly when you didn't want it to.

Lana worried about how hard Savannah had taken being the biggest gossip target in town. Well, Savannah wasn't the one who had done anything wrong, except for maybe trusting a man who wasn't at all trustworthy. Everyone had a past. Sometimes you just had to let go of things and move on.

As soon as their shift was finally over, she headed to the drive-thru section of the bank. "Come on, Savannah. It's dinner time. Let's get a grass fed burger over at CowTown Diner and shake off the work day."

"Ok, sounds good. I'd better text daddy." Savannah said. "He might want me to bring him something."

Lana wiggled her eyebrows. "You bring all the details!"

Savannah laughed. "You bet. Meet you there!"

THE COWTOWN DINER was a little more high-end than the name might suggest. The air smelled like smoked meat and sweet desserts. There was a "Bluegrass money" kind of feel to the place, with its plush leather booths and dark wood trim. Savannah had loved it since it first opened, especially the many paintings of horses on every wall.

As she stuffed her face with sweet potato fries and a bun-less burger smothered in bourbon BBQ sauce, she tried not to make too big a deal of her lunch-time fun with Brody.

"So, aren't you going to ask me about going home for lunch?" Savannah smiled devilishly at her friend. "I DID see Brody Bangfield out at the ranch. Finally!"

"Really? Ooh, what was he doing?"

"Brody Bangfield was in the barn, singing a cowboy song to a sweet little calf, and then -"

Lana interrupted her. "You sure like to say his name. I guess next you'll be writing "Savannah Bangfield" on your notebooks, like you were back in middle school."

"OH, stop! Anyway, he was SINGING and then I sang, too, and then...well... I don't know for sure if I kissed him or if he kissed me... but we KISSED!"

"Already? Wow, you weren't kidding! Was it amazing?"

Savannah just couldn't stop grinning. "AMAZING," she said. "Like, I was seriously forgetting to breathe." She loved sharing her lunch adventure with her best friend.

"SO, he takes your breath away. You better slow it down then. There might be something worthwhile with him," Lana counseled.

"I can't try that whole 'boy meets girl then they live happily ever after' thing. I've been down that stupid road too many times before. It never works, at least for me. I told you I'm just going to have NO STRINGS. Just fun!"

Lana knew that wasn't really Savannah's personality. "But, maybe he is the real deal."

"Oh, what are the odds of that?" Savannah rolled her eyes as she cut another huge bite of her burger and stuffed it into her mouth.

Lana persisted. "Maybe destiny brought him here, from out west, just for you." She poured it on thick, laughing with her friend. "Love and romance, and singing! We've got to have hope, girl!"

"I think hope has been embarrassed right out of me." Savannah suddenly looked very sad.

"I know everybody can't be as lucky as me and Bobby Joe. That man is always trying to make an honest woman out of me," Lana admitted.

"When you gonna' let him marry you?"

"I don't know. I don't want to rock the boat," Lana hedged.

Savannah finished her Maker's Mark and motioned for just one more from the new waitress. "Hope. Ha. Hard to have hope." She started counting reasons on her fingers. "Guys around here act like good guys, trying to win you over, but then their real personality starts showing and they forget to hide their moodiness, or depression… or, their scary bad temper that keeps coming out. Or, they secretly have an affair with someone that goes to church with you!"

Lana laughed while eating Savannah's sweet potato fries. "Right? Then, they want you to make their credit card payment, just this once! Or, they forget to hide all their drug paraphernalia!"

"Or, two of their ex-wives show up!" Savannah knew they were getting louder, but she didn't care.

"With four rowdy children under the age of six!"

"And they start chewing with their mouth open and trimming their beard over the sink and leaving all the little hairs everywhere! And all they can ever say is 'I'M SORRY, BABY' but not like they are sorry at all."

The waitress walked over to them and said, "Or they sleep with your sister after you forgave them for two other women already?" She smiled, laid their check on the table, and backed away.

"Ugh!" Lana fell over in the booth. "Enough! My stomach hurts from laughing."

SAVANNAH ENJOYED THROWING men under the bus with Lana, and it was her life experience that many of them deserved it. She had to admit to herself that she wished Brody Bangfield truly was the real deal, ready to make her world a beautiful place.

She would love to try to make his world a beautiful place, too. Love should be a two-way street.

Was he really the real deal?

She didn't want to get hurt again, so how was she supposed to figure out if that could be true?

CHAPTER 5

*S*aturday mornings were filled with knocking things off the to-do list and marking them off in her big planner. Then she would kick back and relax. That's just the way Savannah was raised. Daddy always said work first and reward yourself later.

She had started her day early and was back from the grocery before most people even woke up and thought about coffee.

After sweeping and mopping the kitchen floor she flipped the laundry and began to fold the sheets while her mind wandered to the bunkhouse. There were a couple of things she needed to do there.

She decided to go there next, before she sweat out her hair. This June was a mix of hot and cool days and today was a hot one - hot enough for cut-off shorts and a Shop Local Kentucky brand tee shirt that said Miss Bourbon. She wanted to look good in case she ran into a certain brawny cowboy.

Savannah saw Brody outside. He looked up as her Honda expertly backed down the gravel drive. She could feel him watching as she popped open the hatchback and hefted a huge bag of dog food up onto her shoulder and headed toward him.

"Morning. Can I help you with that?"

"No, I'm good." she said as she headed around to the bunkhouse back porch.

He rushed to get the door for her and said, "Is this an excuse to come see me?"

"I was doing all of this stuff way before you came along, Brody Bangfield!" she grinned.

She set the dog food down and opened the big tub. Brody slit the top of the bag with his pocket knife and she poured it in. The sound of the dog food filling the tub produced a huge solid black german shepherd at the door immediately.

"Let Cinder in."

Cinder hardly gave Brody a glance and stood right in front of Savannah while turning his head first one way and then the next, trying to figure out which command she would speak first.

"Sit." She gave him a piece of dog food. "Shake. Lay down. Roll over. Good boy! Savannah loves her puppy!" He earned lots of dog food treats.

Brody grinned. "I thought this was Glenwood's dog."

Savannah scratched behind both of Cinder's ears. "Oh, he is, but everybody knows he loves me best."

Brody could sure see why. She looked like the picture of health in her cut-off shorts and brown well-worn cowboy boots. "You seem to be able to handle the biggest bag of dog food like a boss, too," he said.

"Well, anyone can dress like a country girl, but not everyone can work like one," Savannah replied. "Do the country girls in Oklahoma know how to work?"

"I don't know. I was in Montana."

Savannah laughed. "Same difference. Do you like the dog?"

"Very much. He seems crazy smart."

"Oh, he is. His vocabulary is huge. I'm going to miss him when I leave this town."

"Got a new job or something?"

"Nope, not yet. I just need to get away from this town and some bad memories. I'll find a job though, no problem."

"I don't think you need to get in a hurry about that," Brody advised. "That's a big decision."

Savannah liked hearing this from him, and she quickly decided to postpone her other chores for a while, moving into the living room area of the bunkhouse with Cinder at her heels.

Brody followed, taking his beige cowboy hat off.

Savannah loved the lodge decor in this room, with dark woods and big windows with a view of beautiful green fields and fences. "I usually come down here and sweep and mop the kitchen floor on Saturdays. When old Sylvester lived here, he could hardly handle that. He couldn't really see if there were crumbs on the floor anyway."

"It doesn't need it. I'll take care of all that while I'm here."

"Well, you are a very fine employee indeed! We will make you a permanent Kentucky Cowboy before you know it."

"I'll have to keep my Western values," Brody said.

"I think they'll fit right in here in Kentucky."

"You might be right."

She looked around for some reason to not leave yet. She faced the dart board, and grinned. "Got time to help me choose where I'm going when I leave?"

"Maybe..." Brody said.

She opened the desk drawer and unfolded a large map of the United States. With push pins, she hung the map on the cork board wall, covering the dart board. She patted the couch. "Cinder, come. Jump. Stay," she said, so Cinder could watch the action safely.

Brody picked up the darts. "Preference?" he asked.

She took the black and gold, leaving him the black and red.

She backed up and took aim while she said, "Where should I move to?"

She flung the dart with everything she had, a bit to the left. She squinted at the map.

Brody walked over to the map and took a close look. "Paradise, California?"

"Nah, that's no good. I can't deal with Earthquakes."

"And wildfires," he offered.

"High cost of living, too. Ok, your turn." She swept her hand toward him.

Brody took his spot.

"Hey, now, don't cheat the toe line!" Savannah took him by the shoulders and moved him backwards, barely an inch. *Wow, he smells good. And these shoulders feel like warm stone. He is solid as a rock.*

He laughed and focused on trying to hit the map somewhere in the farmlands of Kentucky. He threw the dart and then moved again to the map. "Versailles, Kentucky," he said, saying it like the French.

Savannah fell over onto the couch with the dog and giggled. "Versailles?" She said it like him. "It's Ver- SAILS. And, it's only about 30 minutes away. That's too close."

"Ver- SAILS, huh? Ok… so, it's your turn." He gave her a hand to help her up.

"Thank you." She released his hand reluctantly, took her position, and flung the dart a little closer to home.

He went to look at the board. "Never heard of this one. Screamer, Alabama."

"You are making that up," she said as she went to look for herself.

"I am not. Look," he pointed.

She knew when she came that close that she wanted to kiss him again more than anything on God's green earth. She breathed him in.

Shaking her head, she squinted at the map. "Wow," she got out just as Brody's mouth claimed hers.

Oh! He's kissing me again!

So soon! OH!

Wait until I tell Lana.

Kiss him back, girl!

Savannah found herself moving in closer and giving in to this kiss with everything she had. Time seemed to stand still in the few very delicious moments. Her mind delighted in the chemistry between them.

They were both brought out of their kiss by the very large black German Shepherd, pushing himself between them, and looking up as if to laugh at them, tongue out, and panting.

"How is this not surprising? There's something between us again." Brody shook his head.

Savannah put one hand on the big dog and said, "I told you he loved me best."

"So...I wonder why they call that town Screamer. Bobcats, maybe?" Brody grinned.

"Maybe. I'll have to Google that and get back to you..."

Brody slowly let go of Savannah. "I think we had better get back to our Saturday chores, Savannah, as tempted as I am to chuck them all."

"OK, as long as you promise to think about me - a lot."

Savannah clicked her tongue to Cinder and they went out the door. She wanted to look back to see if Brody was still watching but she didn't let herself.

She did walk with every ounce of feminine swing she could find though, just in case. She knew her legs looked good in shorts and boots.

BRODY WATCHED those long legs taking her back to her car.

"Think about you a lot? No worries about that one, girl."

CHAPTER 6

*B*rody stood at a high point in the field with Glenwood. The smells of summer wafted all around them, with a top note of sweet honeysuckle.

"The field rotations have been working with this number of cattle, so far at least." Glenwood looked out over the rolling north fields from their vantage point. He saw a view of green grass, dotted with cows, as far as the eye could see. This always made the man smile. "I have always loved this view."

"It sure is pretty. The only thing I can think of that would make it look any better is some snow-capped mountains off in the distance," Brody teased.

"Haha," said Glenwood. "Kentucky has some Appalachian hills up near Ashland, if you get to missing them too bad."

Brody took his work gloves off and put them in his back pocket before he opened his notes in his phone. "It is beautiful here, different from the mountains I'm used to, but mighty nice. The adjoining acreage is going to bring your total to what?"

"Let's see... the rented 57 acres brings it to... 297 in grazing land alone," Glenwood said. "I wish there were three more. I like rounded numbers! Now, I'm hoping to talk the owner into eventually selling it to me. We go way back and she doesn't want the horse-racing industry buying up every available Kentucky acre any more than I do."

"The property total?"

"Almost 400 acres."

"That leaves plenty of room to expand the herd with sustainability." Brody made notes in his phone.

"That is the plan. There's only a couple of houses there. One is Mizz Myrtle, the owner. The other is a young woman and her little boy. Mizz Myrtle has been there for decades, still has some cattle but doesn't keep up with things like she should. We've been kind of looking out for her for several years now. It's time she sold that land to me. I've told her she could still stay there."

"That's commendable."

Well, she's been almost like a grandma to my daughter," Glenwood explained.

"I must say Kentucky makes some fine land for cattle."

"Yes, indeed. That new bull, Bruno, has had his mind on expanding the herd since I got him in the spring. He is mean and big as a barn."

Brody was used to big angry bulls. "I bet he eats more than all the others."

"Yep. Anyway, I'm thinking if you like it here and stay on as Master Herdsman, we can increase by 20 to 30 percent in the next couple of years," Glenwood went on.

"I'm leaning in that direction, Glenwood. And it won't take long to get 'Certified Grass Fed Status' either." Brody knew this was the number one goal at the moment.

"Heck, better than that, son - BLUEGRASS Grass Fed status!" Glenwood chuckled at his favorite new joke.

He was feeling better all the time about having reached out to his old friend Scott Bangfield to help fill the Master Herdsman position. This son of Scott's, Brody, was a likable fellow who knew how to work hard and had a long list of solid references. "Let's head to the house and have a shot of Knob Creek?"

"That's another bourbon name?"

"Oh, yes, and I think we've earned the bourbon today."

"I'll never keep them all straight. Maybe I should keep some notes."

Glenwood pointed again to Bruno, the huge bull down in the lower fields. "Brody, I haven't had Bruno long. He's young and seems to be enjoying his ninety day breeding season. You know you should probably never turn your back on him."

"Yeah, I've noticed he seems to have a temper. Calm and deliberate would be the way to go. I'm getting him used to me. He doesn't mind a little pressure from me when I'm on Paulo. He doesn't like when I'm on the ground, so I'll give him plenty of room when he's around his lady cows."

They walked the winding cow path toward the barns. Brody slowed down a little to match Glenwood's slower pace.

"My dad said you two were at University of Kentucky together."

"Did he say he would have never made it through his agriculture degree if it wasn't for me?"

"That's exactly what he said! He needs to slow down these days, but you can't tell him anything."

Glenwood shook his head. "You never could. Now, me? I'm smart enough to know I need to slow down a little, get some good help around here. That's what you are. I don't want to tell Savannah my arthritis bothers me bad when it rains - I'd never hear the end of it! My last Master Herdsman retired on me and moved to Memphis to be near his grandkids, but it was time for him to slow down for sure."

"What was his name again?"

"Sylvester. So, Savannah was mighty glad to see I hired you to take his place. She was afraid I was going to take on too much again."

"She seems to be crazy about you. Daughters are supposed to worry about their dads, right?" Brody opened the two gates by the big barns.

"And so are sons. You worry about your dad, right?"

"I do. Mostly about how he seems to believe in the first-born son inheritance. The whole Jacob and Esau brother thing. My older brother? He could care less about dad's farm, but he talks a big game to dad. That's crazy to me."

"Well, you're not the kind of man to try and steal anyone's birthright. Come on, now. Maybe your dad will rethink that. Or, maybe you'll build a life here to be proud of," Glenwood chuckled. "Also... maybe you shouldn't mention my complaining about my arthritis to Savannah... I don't want her to stay around here just for me if she's decided she wants to move away. I'd never guilt her into not doing what she wants to do."

"Of course."

"Then again, she doesn't always know what she wants to do. Women."

They both laughed at that.

As they reached the wraparound porch of the main house, Cinder stood up from the shadows and leaned against Glenwood, who reached down to rub the dog's broad sides.

Four big hanging potted ferns moved slightly in the breeze and the shade of the porch felt good to the two men.

"BRODY, step into the house and pour the Knob's Creek for me." The older man sat down in the white oak rocker while Cinder lay at his feet.

It had been a good day, hot, with a few clouds here and there. It was time to kick back after a long day's work.

Glenwood shifted his aching hip in the rocking chair and sighed.

Savannah would be home from the bank soon. She would dish up whatever it was she had thrown into the crockpot before she left this morning. Maybe it was a chuck roast with potatoes and carrots. You could smell it out here on the porch and it smelled good.

Lord, help me to notice all the good things in my life. Amen

Now, if he could just get in some subtle match-making, he could call this day done. He started to imagine grandchildren running around the yard, laughing like Savannah and smiling like Brody.

Hey, it was worth a shot.

"And this time add just a couple of ice cubes to them, ok?" He called through the screen door.

"No problem, sir."

Brody came out the door and handed Glenwood a glass as he sat down on the top step. "Do you mind if I ask why your daughter is thinking about leaving here?"

Glenwood drank his fine bourbon and looked out across his beloved land. "I don't know how she could leave this place - most of this land has been in our family since 1927. But, I guess that's really her story to tell ya, Brody. She would tell me a different reason every time I ask."

Brody shook his head and finished his bourbon. He stood up and smiled at Glenwood and handed the man his empty glass back. "Fair enough. Thanks for the drink. I like this one, Knob's Creek."

"One more thing - I don't think I've mentioned the big event coming up at the end of the month. We always host a Kentucky Young Farmers Day. It's an event for local kids and I'm gonna need all hands for that."

"That sounds like fun," said Brody.

"It will be the Young Farmer boys you're getting to know every Thursday, plus about a hundred other people. Mostly young families with their kids in tow."

"What will you need me to do?"

"Oh, well, ask Savannah where you're needed most. She always has a whole Happy Planner on the event." Glenwood's eyes twinkled.

"Happy? Planner?"

"Oh, yeah. It's a thing. Full of plans and different colored stickers and happy… stuff."

"Yeah? Well, I'll make sure she puts me in that happy planner."

"That sounds real good to me. Here's her phone number." He showed Brody the number on his phone. "Oh, hey, you a church goer?"

"Actually, I was going to ask you about that. I am going to want to find a church to be involved in," Brody said as he put the number into his phone.

Glenwood winked at Brody. "Good. Ask Savannah for a recommendation on that, too."

As BRODY WALKED to the bunkhouse, he wondered what that wink meant. It seemed like maybe Mr Stetson was trying to say more than he was actually saying. Anyway, Brody was happy to have any reason to talk to the intriguing Miss Savannah Stetson.

Now, he had two good reasons.

CHAPTER 7

*S*avannah heard a horn blow just outside the house. She slid her feet into her sandals and grabbed her purse as she hurried to lock the door behind herself.

"Hey."

Lana could barely be seen over the steering wheel of Bobby Joe's big truck - army green with padded camo fender flares - this truck was Bobby Joe's baby. She grinned as Savannah opened the door and swung herself up and into the seat.

"Something wrong with your car?"

Lana laughed. "No, I just didn't know how much we might be buying on this trip."

"Lots. We will be buying more stuff than daddy will think we need."

Lana laughed. "Seriously, Bobby Joe thought my brakes sounded funny, so he's checking it out."

"He's a keeper." Savannah pulled her planner out of her purse and found her list. "See why I hang out with you? Daddy knows we need a lot of supplies for the Kentucky Young Farmers Day, especially snacks and drinks and poster supplies -

some of the kids won't have their own stuff. So, how about coffee first, then we bang through this day!"

Savannah never missed an opportunity to get coffee or to make it herself. Coffee was her favorite.

Lana looked over at her friend. "It keeps hitting me - who am I going to do all this stuff with if you move to the big city? You sure you could even find a decent man there?"

"Awww. Just drive, ok? Change is so hard. I don't want to think about it right now. You know I'm just so tired of being hurt. If I could have found real, lasting love in this little town, wouldn't I have done it by NOW?"

Lana put it into gear and kept the conversation light for the rest of the drive to the coffee shop drive-through.

Just as they pulled into the warehouse grocery parking lot, Savannah's phone rang. She barely glanced down at it.

"Everyone I know texts me - not important."

"Answer it!"

"They can leave a message. I don't know this number."

"What if it's Brody?" Lana batted her eyelashes made a heart with her hands.

Savannah's eyes were wide. "OH! Ok." Into the phone she said, "Hello, this is Savannah."

"Hey. It's Brody."

Savannah's eyes got wider as she mouthed "It IS Brody." She put him on speaker phone and that made Lana's eyes widen, too. "What's up?"

"I was just talking to Mr Stetson and he brought up the Kentucky Young Farmers Day for kids. I told him I'd be happy to help any way I can."

"I think that's great! Thank you." Savannah loved where this was going. She also loved that Brody sounded just a little bit nervous talking to her.

"Your dad said you would need to put me in your happy

planner...so... I wanted to offer to help you with that... happy... planning, any way I can."

"Well, Brody, I'll have to think about where I can put "Brody Bangfield" in my Happy Planner... for the best bang for my buck, right?" Savannah shot Lana a look and nearly laughed out loud.

Lana put her hand over her mouth so she wouldn't laugh out loud.

"I don't know enough about the event yet, but surely there are things I can help with."

"I can think of a few things, yes." By this time she was about to giggle, and Lana did laugh out loud.

Brody heard it and paused. "Savannah Stetson, am I on speaker phone?"

"Yes, and Lana and I are shopping for supplies for the big event right now. I really am glad to have another volunteer though. Are you good with kids?" She had a feeling he was.

"Better than you might imagine."

"I had one more thing to ask you about but I think I'll wait until I see you. Text me, now that you have my number, if there's a day this week I can bring you lunch to the bank? We can talk about where I will be the most help."

Savannah sighed. "That would be wonderful. Now, say bye to Lana."

"Bye, Lana."

Lana was still cracking up at them. "Bye, Brody!"

THE GIRLS HOPPED down from the truck and headed toward the shopping carts.

"Let's get a buggy." Lana started pulling one out of the line.

"Let's get a cart!" Savannah laughed. They always giggled about calling the carts different things. Little things like this connected their memories through the years, reminding them that they were like sisters in so many ways. Lana had tried to get her interested in each of her four brothers, but that never worked. The brothers had always been more like annoying family than someone to flirt with.

Putting themselves in high gear and rolling on caffeine, they had everything on the list they needed in under 30 minutes, including all kinds of extras for the poster-making area. They also loaded up on balloons, tablecloths, and crepe paper streamers in red and white.

They got extra bottled waters for the older kids' speech-practice section. The upcoming scholarship competitions made this part of the day crucial. Practice helped calm the nerves.

"I think we are in pretty good shape here, considering," Lana said as she put items back into the cart at the check-out.

Savannah thought so, too. "Well, it would help if we knew the weather, and how many people will actually show up but that's too much to ask. I've already got cotton candy, popcorn, and snow cone machines booked for the day, too."

"You can count on the hayride guy, too," Lana said, referring to Bobby Joe.

"He's a keeper."

"Yes, most days he is."

Back in the truck, Lana teased her friend a little more.

"You did not flirt at all with our check-out fellow, and he was so cute."

"Was he? I didn't even notice."

"Hmmm. He was tall, dark, and handsome. Were you too busy thinking about Brody again?"

"Well, yes! I wonder if he would do best with; the petting zoo, explaining all about the new calves and all that? Or, he might be good with helping the older kids practice their speeches? He's, you know, smart and patient. I don't know yet. Maybe I'll have a better idea after he brings me lunch at the bank."

Lana rolled her eyes but didn't interrupt. "You go on and on about Brody Bangfield. That might keep you from wasting time chasing after the wrong boys, which isn't like the real you at all!"

Savannah smiled. "I know. I know."

"Heck fire, it might even keep you from leaving town. Now, wouldn't that be perfect?" Lana laughed.

"It actually might. Remember when you thought it would be perfect if your brother Malachi was my boyfriend? What was that? Eighth grade?"

Lana shook her head. "Maybe seventh grade. I should have known he was too shy and quiet for you. I think I tried to get Creed and Eli both to notice you in eighth grade."

LATER THAT NIGHT, as Savannah was propped up in bed with her journal, she thought back on the times in her life when she had been excited about getting to know a new guy. Things were always exciting and shiny new at the beginning. Guys were always on their best behavior when they were trying to win you over.

Savannah loved the time just before falling asleep, the time of relaxing thoughts and sometimes magnificent insights. Tonight her mind was going in circles. Monkey brain, that's what she had.

Men, ugh, always wanting to impress you at first, being all happy and helpful and attractive but then they cheat on you with someone from your church or something! I can't be getting all excited just because Brody is gorgeous and fit and makes my toes curl up and then stretch out again when we kiss.

I can't get too close to him.

I can't get attached. I can't.

He has some kind of power to make my heart thump.

I need to stay far away from that kind of trouble.

Oh, but her heart wasn't listening. It was thumping away in a double-time rhythm while she tried to write in her journal. Her heart had a mind of its own, and she could feel it building deep feelings for a certain reliable cowboy.

So, she gave in and texted Brody this message: "How about lunch Wednesday?"

It took a long time to go to sleep after that.

CHAPTER 8

*E*ven though it seemed like Wednesday would never come, it finally did.

Savannah mindlessly worked the bank duties on Wednesday morning while her imagination made flirty conversation with Brody. She had dressed nicer than usual for today and had curled her hair, but the sky was threatening a downpour.

Stupid rain. Hold off! I want to have lunch outside, on the picnic table beside the bank! Maybe no one else will be out there today; that'll be perfect. We can talk about the Kid's Day event and I can ask him about ranching stuff, too.

There's his truck! It really matches him, all solid and dependable.

She grabbed her purse and planner and walked toward the door, hoping to head him off before he even got into the bank lobby. Diamond Rio's Meet In the Middle started playing above her head as she watched Brody walk toward her in the bank's lot.

Wow, his gait exactly matches the tempo of that good ole' song, with that belt buckle riding along, in no hurry at all. He is full of confidence and swagger!

She began to sing that song as she started walking his way.

She loved the way it made him look at her as she went through the door.

Brody grinned as he held up four red and white bags from her favorite fast food chicken place. "Hey. Hope you're hungry, little songbird."

"I love Diamond Rio. Let's sit at that picnic table, at least until the rain makes us run for it, ok?"

"Sure. I didn't know what your lunch order would be from the drive-through, so I got lots of stuff. We didn't have these chicken places out west. So, you can pick first and I'll eat the rest! Sweet tea or Lemonade?"

"Sweet tea. Thank you - that's so sweet of you. Ha!"

They sat down on the same side of the picnic table and she liked that since it put them closer together. "We're sitting on the same side, so we won't have a picnic table between us, right?"

"For sure," he laughed. "How's your day going?"

"It's blah. Same old thing - other people's money. Lana's off today, too, so that makes it seem longer."

She pulled out a southwest salad, thirty nuggets with sauce, waffle fries, two sandwiches, two cookies, and a yogurt parfait. "Wow. Let's just share it all!"

"Well, I like that plan."

They worked on the food for a while in silence. Before it got awkward she jumped in. "How's the job? Isn't Daddy just the best?"

"He knows how to get things done, that's for sure. He is keeping me on my toes. We're working on a plan to reach 'Certified Biodynamic Pasture' so he can advertise the beef and the calves on sites that cater to people searching for that. He's got a solid start, so I don't think it's going to take us long to grow a larger calf crop.

"Now, I've got some ideas about how to lose less weight on the hoof right before they go to market, too.

"Wait. Am I boring you with ranch details?"

"Of course not. I even know what you're talking about. We treat our herds pretty well, and that is a rock-solid financial decision. You might be surprised to know that I can work a herd of cattle by myself with Buttercup. I just don't want to do it all the time."

"Nice! So, is that the planner I heard about?" Brody gestured to it with a huge waffle fry dipped in golden sauce. "It's...big."

"It is, but there's a lot to keep up with."

"Like the Kentucky Young Farmers thing?"

"Oh. Yeah." She flipped a few pages. "I can make a copy of our tentative schedule for you. I think you could help with check-in, then work in the barns with telling groups about a day in the life of the calves on our farm; that's right before the tour guides would take them to the petting area. Then, would you care to listen to some of the agriculture speeches after the lunch break? It's practice for a college scholarship competition, and some of them really need positive practice."

Brody could see how invested she was in the kids so he said, "Yes. Yes, to all of it."

Suddenly, huge raindrops started hitting the planner. "Oh!"

Both of them grabbed up everything on the picnic table and Brody pulled out his keys. "Let's make a run for the truck!"

Even with everything they were carrying he managed to hold her hand as they dashed across the alleyway to the side parking lot.

Rain came down so hard and fast it had nowhere to go.

Lightening crawled across the sky as they piled into Brody's big red Ford. Thunder crashed just as a familiar big white truck drove by throwing water up in all directions. The driver kept hitting the horn in short repetitive blasts.

"Wow. I shouldn't have bothered to curl my hair this morning..." Savannah said while checking her phone and completely ignoring the noisy truck. "I've got 10 more minutes."

The white truck screeched around the corner.

"I'll drop you off right at the door, don't worry. Now, where'd those cookies wind up?" He found a cookie, took a big bite, and offered her one.

The noisy white truck was circling the parking lot slowly now. Inside was a guy in a John Deere cap, staring at them.

"Well, now, that's rude. What is he looking at?" Brody asked.

Savannah was suddenly uncomfortable. "Oh, it might be an ex-boyfriend. He is rude, for sure."

"Well, if he drives by again, I'm going to plant a big kiss on you. Give him something to look at! Get ready."

Savannah realized she wasn't uncomfortable anymore. "Thanks for the warning. But, what if my mouth is stuffed with chocolate chip cookie?" She leaned in close to him.

"Oh, that won't stop me. Might be fun."

Savannah took a big bite and reached for his shirt. She pulled him closer so they could kiss away the last few minutes before she had to get back into the bank. She never did notice if Randy Haner drove by again or not. Her mind was overtaken with butter and sugar and dark chocolate chunks and kissing and licking her lips in this strange but delicious cookie-kiss.

She might have even forgotten all about getting back to work and been late, but somehow the gentleman cowboy remembered reality. He slowly stopped kissing her and smiled into her eyes as he rubbed a bit of chocolate off of the corner of her mouth.

"Best cookie ever." His voice had a husky depth.

"No way. I make the best cookies," she whispered.

This man is just too delicious for words.

He dropped her off at the door, right on time. "Your hair looks beautiful, even though you got rained on. Thanks for a perfect lunch."

Savannah gave her best smile as she hopped down from his truck. "Thank YOU for a perfect lunch."

CHAPTER 9

*B*rody placed his speed rope at his feet near the outdoor pull-up bar and started to set his timer. Everything was ready for a workout that might help clear his head.

Cinder ran up and dropped a worn tennis ball at his feet. The dog watched him expectantly, ready to chase after the ball.

"You want to be part of this workout, yeah?" He gave the ball a mighty pitch across the big backyard.

Three. Two. One. Go! The timer beeped the countdown.

Brody's pull-ups were fast and efficient. He knew his mind could wander at will during this "As Many Rounds as Possible" session. He wanted to try to figure out why he found Savannah so unbelievably interesting. Maybe then he could stop thinking about her constantly.

She was smart and beautiful and funny, but lots of women were. Why did she completely invade his thoughts and just take up residence there?

He grabbed a deep breath and picked up the rope. His double-unders made a satisfying whirring sound as he mindlessly counted them off.

He hadn't been this interested in a woman in a long time. Maybe it was just timing that made her so irresistible. She was here. He was here. She was new. She was fun to kiss with chocolate chip cookies! Heck, she was even organized and a hard worker.

He dropped the rope, threw the ball for Cinder again, and went back to the pull-ups.

He kept catching himself imagining their future together, building a home, and a family, and holidays and... what in the world was he thinking about all of that stuff for, anyway? Maybe Kentucky sunshine was making him soft.

These thoughts were making it hard for him to count his reps.

He'd have to check with Glenwood to see if he could have a dog of his own here. Savannah probably loved puppies and Cinder might enjoy having a sidekick. Brody had always had a dog and Kentucky would feel more like home if he did.

He wondered if he would settle here for sure. If he did, he would need to make a trip out west and get his horse and bring him here, or at least sell him. He could get in a visit with his dad and mom, and try to avoid his brother.

He did not need to hear his brother brag about how he was the best at everything, how much money he'd made, or how many women were in love with him. All of that was old news, and highly predictable.

The gentle lowing of the nearby cows seemed to lull him into slowing down his workout. He'd better have some energy left in the tank for riding over the far North corner this afternoon anyway. He would need to count the herds and switch them to other fields. He might as well keep an eye on the fence line, too, on the perimeter of the properties.

What was the story with Savannah's old boyfriend in the white truck, driving by more than once? That was enough to make a man feel territorial; protective, even. Brody always tried to see the best in people but he had a bad feeling about that fellow.

Maybe Savannah would tell him about it when she trusted him more.

A man could dream. He sure had been doing a lot of that lately. Any man would be lucky to be the one she shared her thoughts with...

Cinder nudged him out of his thoughts with a slobbery ball against his leg.

"Oh, sorry, bud. Give me the ball. Last throw, ok?"

He smiled as Cinder raced a few yards across the grassy area and looked back at him, alert and ready.

Brody would be at the ready, too, whenever Savannah needed him. The idea of that made him feel happy and hopeful as he quickly coiled his speed rope.

He threw the ball and took off toward the bunkhouse.

CHAPTER 10

*S*avannah threw her purse and keys on the hallway table and made her way to the kitchen, kicking off her shoes along the way. It had been a long day. She started flipping through the mail laying on the table.

"Hey, Daddy."

Glenwood was at the breakfast nook with a turkey sandwich and sweet tea. "Oh, howdy. Before I forget, I told Brody he should talk to you about a church recommendation when I saw him earlier." Glenwood grinned at his daughter.

"Daddy! Seriously?" She tried to give her dad a stern look.

"Yes, seriously. I think it's a wonderful thing that a nice young man, new in town, would even ask about church. Brody is growing on me. He growing on you?" He grinned at her and wiggled his eyebrows.

Savannah shrugged her shoulders.. Thinking about church made her nervous since she broke up with Randy Haner a couple of months ago. "Daddy, why?"

"Why what?"

"Oh, never mind. Look, Brody brought me lunch at the bank

today and he didn't mention church at all." She reached over and took a bite of her dad's sandwich.

"Huh. He seemed like he was interested. Works so hard. Fine young man," Glenwood poured it on thick.

"Yeah. I recently thought a son of a preacher-man was a fine young man, too. Remember? You just can't always tell," Savannah poured herself a sweet tea. "What are y'all working on tomorrow, afternoon when the KYF boys are here?"

"Weeding the corn field, feeding the calves, setting out a few more tomatoes and staking them. You got time to make them some snacks?"

"I'm thinking I can do dinner tomorrow."

"Aw, they'll love that. Count Brody in, too, ok?" he said as he grabbed up his farm magazines and hightailed it out of the kitchen before she gave him something to do.

"No problem, dad."

THURSDAY AFTERNOON WAS warm with a slight breeze, so Savannah decided to set up the food in the screened-in back porch. The porch was as long as the entire back of the house and made a great place to feed people. She had been making cookies and sandwiches and bowls of soup for teen-aged "help" for years now with the Kentucky Young Farmers.

Her dad had a heart as big as the Bluegrass State when it came to kids who didn't have much parental support - if the boys wanted to come and work on Thursdays, then daddy always found jobs for them, and a little pay, too. The names of the boys changed, but the idea was the same - give those boys a man to look up to. That way they could learn how to work hard and appreciate the importance of farm-life.

Savannah smiled. She guessed she was like her dad in that respect. She enjoyed Thursday afternoons and didn't mind helping out. She never had much trouble keeping the fellows from trying to flirt with her - they were way too young for her to put up with that.

Lately, all she could think about was trying to flirt with Brody at every opportunity, and no wonder, with all that fitness underneath his clothes, and his polite and thoughtful ways.

Her mind wandered back to lunch yesterday after they made a dash for his truck. The rain made it so cozy and intimate in the truck. She would never look at a Chick-fil-A chocolate chip cookie the same way again. Yum.

She checked her phone. The boys would be finishing up soon, so she started setting out everything that could go on a burger: cheeses, smokey BBQ sauce, bacon she had just taken out of the oven, pickles, and lettuce. No tomatoes yet - if they weren't summer tomatoes, they weren't worth eating and late June was too early for that.

She went to the fridge for the deviled eggs she had made. They would be delicious with the potato salad she had picked up from the CowTown Diner.

What else?

She never thought she had enough food, and the funny thing was, with teenage boys, however much you had was how much they ate. You could never fill up growing boys.

As she went back into the kitchen for potato chips, paper plates, ketchup, and mustard, she heard them heading her way when she reached the back porch.

"Hi, guys. Y'all come on in. Who's hungry?" That's all she had to say.

They all lined up to make their plates when Leon, a quiet teenager said, "You mind if we bless the food before we eat it?"

She smiled. "Go right ahead, Leon." She looked over their heads and smiled at Brody, who had just come through the screen door. She made prayer hands so he would know to bow his head.

Leon bowed his head, and cleared his throat. "Dear Lord, thank you for this food to nourish our bodies. We all sure appreciate it. And, thank you for Mr. Stetson letting us come out and work. And, God, look down and bless pretty Savannah, too. In Jesus' precious name, Amen."

He'd always had a little crush on Savannah. Now it seemed like it was showing up in his prayers.

The other boys laughed at the end of that prayer as Glenwood swatted Leon with his cowboy hat.

Leon said, "I'm sorry, sir! Her eyes are just so soulful, like a baby calf. No offense, ma'am." He shrugged his bony shoulders.

"None taken, Leon."

After everyone had finished eating their meal, the boys offered to clean up and put things away. Savannah didn't waste any time taking them up on it so she could talk to Brody.

She turned to him. "Let's take a walk so you can show me what y'all accomplished today?"

"I'd be honored," Brody said.

Savannah ignored Glenwood's grin and the boys elbowing each other as Brody held the screen door open for her.

As they walked together to the garden, Brody said, "I had a good time watching your dad with those Young Farmer boys. They hang on his every word."

"He's trying to make sure the world has people who know how to work on a farm and grow their own food. They're always a good group. Daddy knows how to pick them."

The garden was a pretty sight. The color differences stood out in the rows of butter crunch lettuce and dwarf romaine alongside the purple hues in the red romaine. The rainbow blend bell peppers hadn't reached their color peeks yet, but would be showing off very soon. The yellow and orange Inca marigolds brightened up the corners of the big garden. The rows of bean plants, tied to stakes, and the corn made up the tallest section. You could practically see them getting taller each and every day in this part of the summer.

Savannah grinned at Brody. "Nothing much better than fresh corn from the garden."

"Oh, I can't wait," he said.

"You ever eat bacon-wrapped corn on the cob?"

"Whoa, that sounds amazing. By the way, your dad said maybe you could help me figure out a couple of churches to try around here," Brody said.

"Oh, I guess I could do that. Let's see. Close by?" Savannah fidgeted.

"Yep, not too far away. A church needs to be handy, right?"

"Ok, what kind of church did you go to in Oklahoma?" Savannah asked, trying to get a feel for his church preferences.

Brody laughed. "Montana," he said. "Anyway, my church there felt like a real church, you know? I learned a lot, and the music was a good mix. People were busy doing things that brought blessings to others." He picked up a rock laying in the garden dirt and gave it a pitch into the field.

"Well, that helps." Savannah sighed. "Does it need to be a certain type of church for you? What denomination was the one you went to before?"

"Baptist."

"Oh," Savannah chuckled dryly. "Well, you could try the First Baptist Church of Please Don't Make Me Go There." Savannah shook her head with a grimace, picked up a rock and threw it much harder than Brody had.

"There must be a story there!" Brody laughed.

Savannah loved the deep sound of his laugh and that made her more comfortable with this part of her recent history. Maybe talking about it with Brody would make her feel better.

Maybe. Maybe not.

They walked toward the creek branch and sat on a couple of big rocks, side by side, while Brody perfectly imitated the whippoorwill song in the trees above them. She wished she could whistle like that. "Wow. Do you talk to all animals, or is it just birds?"

Brody smiled. "I am pretty good at calming most animals."

He was calming to be around. That was true. She just hadn't realized it yet, since he also made her heartbeat kick up like no one else had ever done.

Savannah couldn't believe it, but she found herself telling him about Randy Haner, her ex-boyfriend. "Oh, there is quite a story connected to that church. I don't know why you'd want to hear this story. I don't even know why I feel like I can tell you about it. It's hard. It's hard to be pointed out in town when you're trying to get groceries, or whispered about in church."

Brody only said, "I can imagine."

She went on. "I'd left the church that I'd gone to off and on for years with daddy. I'd started dating the 'son-of-a-preacher-man' from that church. Have you ever heard of preacher's kids being kind of rotten?"

"Yeah, but only in the movies." He waited for her to continue.

"Well, this one swept me off my feet, played a good game at first, and even wanted to wait until we might someday get married to get intimate. I thought that was so nice, so good. My gut sometimes thought something was off, but he was on such good behavior and I hadn't had a steady boyfriend in a long while. I didn't realize at the time that I didn't feel like getting in a hurry with this relationship, either." She pushed her hair back out of her face. "Well, it turned out that…"

Her voice drifted away and all you could hear were the frogs singing down by the water's edge.

He scooted closer to her on the rocks. "Hey, now, you don't

have to tell me anything. I'm a real good listener and all, but don't feel like you have to."

"No, I need to say it out loud. Maybe you can understand why I don't know what I'm doing lately when it comes to men, or my future, or where I should be living, or anything!" She paused, then took a deep breath and let it all come out in a rush.

"Ok. Randy Haner had been having an affair with a married woman and I knew her and we had all been going to the same church together. They got caught, at the church. At the church! Can you believe that? Then, it was all anyone could talk about - Poor Little Savannah."

"That's really unfair to you, little darling. I'm so sorry."

"Thanks. So, I lost a boyfriend, a friend, and a church I really liked all at the same time, too. Oh, and some of my confidence."

Savannah could tell that Brody was trying to cheer her up when he said, "Wasn't it better to find out when you did, instead of later on when things might have been more serious?"

"I guess it was." She hadn't looked at it that way.

"Sometimes you can stay too long in a relationship, hoping it will get better. I know all about that." He paused. "Did you love him?"

Savannah shook her head. "I think I thought I did, but I didn't. And after it all blew up, I thought he would just calm down and get over it, and leave me alone. But he still drives by in that stupid tricked out noisy truck sometimes, just to make me feel stalked."

Brody sat up a little straighter. "Wait a minute. That guy that drove by, while we were having lunch? At the bank?"

Savannah nodded. "I wish he would just go away."

Brody smiled at the gorgeous woman beside him and felt his heart tug with protectiveness. "Hmm. Maybe the two of us should go to THAT church this Sunday, arm in arm. You want to? I'll make sure every head turns in that church and tongues will be wagging with a new story."

"Awww, I bet they would!" Savannah laughed. "Thanks, but no thanks. The last thing in the world I want to do is rile him up. So." Savannah was ready to change the subject.

"So?" Brody asked.

"Should we start with the church I used to go to? Pleasant Hillside Baptist Church." She suddenly liked the idea of going to her home church with Brody.

"That's a mighty fine name for a church."

"Isn't it?" She thought for a minute. "There's also a fairly new one that Lana goes to now and then. Young preacher. Praise band is supposed to be all rock and roll Jesus."

Brody pushed his cowboy hat back and kissed her on the forehead. "Let's do one this week and one next week, ok? That's two dates."

"Sounds good."

Dates! He said dates! I now have two church dates with Mr Gorgeous Cowboy! Go, Savannah! I feel so brave I think I'll just kiss him again!

"Daddy's going to be way too happy about all of this. You want to kiss me now, or something more?" She smiled slyly.

Brody chuckled. "I hope you don't try to throw yourself at every cowboy that comes along. They might not all be as gentlemanly as me."

"Sometimes I want to just throw myself at you - to prove that I can." She sighed again, wondering how in the world the fates had dropped this reliable cowboy into her life, just when she was getting used to being alone. At the very least, she had planned to just play the field for a while.

Brody put his arm around her shoulders. "Well, if we are lucky, maybe that day will come. But think about what your heart is really chasing after, Savannah. We've got to want the things of Heaven more than the things of this world."

Savannah stood up, took his hand, and pulled him to his feet.

"Ok. Sunday School is at 9:45 and church at 11. You don't have to dress up unless you want to. I'll be ready at 9:15."

How could holding hands make her this happy?

She didn't let go of that big strong hand as she headed up the path toward the house, and she had to work real hard not to skip with happiness.

CHAPTER 11

*S*avannah looked up every time the door opened. This place was packed with hungry people, but she finally saw the one she had been waiting for.

Lana slid into the booth at the CowTown diner and put a sweet potato fry into her mouth. "Hey!" she said around a mouthful of food.

Savannah grinned. "Hey. You are so late I went ahead and ordered. I was starving!" It had only been fifteen minutes, but this girl had to eat. "I ordered the favorite, for you, too."

"Oh, you are awesome."

Savannah smiled. "It just must be genetic. Look. Here comes your food, from yet another new waitress." She moved her phone off the table as the new girl sat down Lana's food. "Thanks."

"Such perfect timing!"

"That's right. I won't have to guard my sweet potato fries!"

"What'd I miss at work?"

"Nothing. Same old, same old. Missed you though," Savannah mumbled around a huge bite.

"How's it going with the plan to leave this great little town and be a girl with a different date every night?" Savannah knew Lana was looking for a specific answer.

"Oh, if I move away, then you'll have to come visit lots. But, I might not be in such a hurry anymore..." Her face lit up like the sun breaking through the clouds on a hot August Lake Cumberland afternoon. "You will be especially happy to know that I am going to Pleasant Hillside on Sunday morning."

"You're going back to church? With your dad?" Lana asked while she quickly ordered a shot of Basil Hayden's bourbon from the new waitress, who didn't seem to know anything about bourbon yet. She would learn quick enough.

"Nope. I'm going with... Brody." Lana nearly knocked her water over as Savannah filled her friend in on their plan to try a few churches for the next few weeks. She also told her about Brody offering to take her to the 'First Baptist Church of Please Don't Make Me Go There' and make sure everyone noticed them together.

"Oh, that would be awesome!" Lana said. "I think you should do it! Maybe that little jerk would stop driving by the bank all the time."

"No, thank you."

"If you ever decide to do it, I want to be there!" Lana put more smoked sea salt on her burger.

"I don't want to do it. I'm wondering why I want to go to church at all, even though I like Pleasant Hillside Church...and Brody." Savannah frowned. "It's making me kind of nervous. Second thoughts, I guess."

"Well, that's because you like Brody so much. You've got to give him a chance! He seems to be a straight-up good guy, and he likes you, and he's helpful and so handsome. Don't you think so?"

Savannah laughed. "He is. He's sure got you won over. I just worry that I'm jumping in too fast; that I like him so much already. Even great men are just so much trouble." Savannah winked at her friend. "So much trouble."

Lana shook her head. "Don't be silly. You've been saying that since the 7th grade and you still don't mean it! What are you going to wear? Oh! Wear that teal and coral sundress and those matching Ariat cowboy boots!"

"Ok. That way I won't have to go shopping."

"And curl your hair."

"That's a lot to ask," Savannah said, but she knew she would curl her hair for her first church service with Brody.

Brody woke earlier than usual on Sunday morning. He drank his black coffee and cleaned his best boots in the backyard of the bunkhouse. He wished he had time to saddle up old Paulo, his favorite of Glenwood's horses. A fast ride would clear his head and settle him. Maybe he could do that later in the afternoon.

Why was he fidgeting so much about taking Savannah to church this morning? He had a feeling it was a big step for her to get back into a church at all after the fiasco with that ex-boyfriend. Wow. How could anyone treat her like that?

Brody knew by now, deep in his bones, that this girl was the one. He couldn't pinpoint exactly when he knew but it was there, an undercurrent in his every breath now. He had thought he could be alone for the rest of his days until he laid eyes on Savannah Kay Stetson.

He looked out across the fields and put one knee on the ground.

He prayed, "Good morning, Lord. Thank you for this glorious day. I don't know why I took this job here in Kentucky on a whim and walked away from everything that I knew. I'm thinking it might be so I could find Savannah. Keep me listen-

ing, Lord, and make today go well. Help me to find the right life.
I'm ready for that. Amen."

Cinder came bounding around the corner as Brody was
heading into the bunkhouse.

He whistled for the big black dog. "Hey, handsome. I'm
going to see our favorite girl this morning. Aren't you happy for
me?" He scratched behind Cinder's velvety black ears. "Wish me
luck, good boy."

He smiled up at the blue Kentucky sky and knew a moment
of staggeringly real happiness.

SAVANNAH WAS ready early and watching out the window for
Brody. She smiled then stood up and checked her hair in the
mirror for the third time as she heard his truck coming up the
driveway. Dropping her planner in her suede-fringed purse, she
went out the door.

Brody got out of the truck and walked around. "Beautiful
morning. You look so pretty." He opened the door of his big red
Ford and shut the door after she got in.

"Hey. You look pretty, too. So, dad went out for a men's
coffee meeting earlier. He's on patrol at church this morning. I
don't know if he will be in the control room or walking the
grounds, but he's already there." She grinned as Brody headed
toward the main road.

"You tell him we're going to be there this morning?"

"Oh, heck, no! I didn't want to hear him tease me. You know
where you're going?"

Brody looked over at Savannah. "Yes, ma'am. Google and I
did our homework." He reached out and squeezed her hand.

"Nice! Now get your eyes on the road."

"Your dress and cowboy boots almost match the interior of
my truck. It's distracting, in a good way."

"Aw, thank you."

Savannah noticed The Pleasant Hillside Baptist Church parking lot wasn't full yet as Brody pulled into a parking space. She had butterflies in her stomach. *Settle down, girl. It's just another Sunday morning in June.*

She noticed Brody had a black tooled leather bible with his name on it. It looked well-used. Somehow this made her ridiculously happy.

She asked Brody, "After Singles Sunday School class, do you want the back row, or would you rather sit in the balcony?"

"Lower level, if that's ok with you. More people can see us together that way."

She was laughing as they went in the doors.

LATER, as they were leaving the service, Savannah could see more than a few women checking Brody out without even trying to hide it. That made her feel happy yet a little uncomfortable and vulnerable. This man - wow, the attraction was a living thing between them and she hoped she could handle things on his timeline. She realized that the longer they waited to get any closer than a few kisses, the more intense the feelings would be.

The church members always spilled out the doors and talked with each other when the weather was nice. People laughed and children ran around the adults in circles.

Beulah Burton, who owned the CowTown Diner, marched right up to Brody. She was wearing a blue and gold suit made out of what looked like gleaming tapestry fabric. Her matching shoes and jewels twinkled in the sun.

Ignoring Savannah completely, she shook his hand and didn't let go. "Howdy, partner. I just wanted to introduce myself and welcome you to our church. I'd love to introduce my daughter, but she's not here this morning. Her name is Miss Annabelle Burton. She will be here next week though, and I want you to stay after church for the after-church dinner so you can taste her famous apple pie. It's the best anywhere around."

Brody got his hand back and said, "Well, thank you, Ms. Burton. Savannah and I will be on the lookout for it if we are here next week." He smiled at both ladies and put his arm around Savannah's waist.

Savannah felt the trust growing between them and she smiled and waved as Beulah walked away. "Tell Annabelle we missed her," she said quietly.

Then she saw her daddy coming down the steps.

She headed toward him and kissed him on the cheek. "Morning. Good sermon, huh?"

"Like always. Brody, good to see you here with my girl. Hope to see you here next week, too." He shook Brody's hand. "I saw Ms Burton didn't want to let go of you. I won't even shake her hand anymore. She likes to hang on, and then you smell like lilac or rosewater all day."

They all laughed at that.

"Daddy could tell you a couple of good stories about Beulah Burton trying to get his attention," Savannah added.

"Let's save that for another day." Glenwood hunted for his keys in his pocket.

"Sir, we'd planned to try a few more churches, but we'll have to talk about that. I really like it here. How can you not love a church with a name like Pleasant Hillside?" Brody grinned.

Glenwood headed slowly down the last of the steps, then looked back at them, holding tight to the railing. "Now, remember, you have the day off. Have fun, you two!"

CHAPTER 12

*S*avannah rode her horse, Buttercup, while Brody rode Paulo with a picnic basket tied onto the back of the saddle. They moved slowly on the path down by the lower branch of Bourbon Creek.

Earlier, they'd packed up some lunch together and decided to make the most of the perfect summer Sunday weather. She had changed from her dress to jeans and a belt with her biggest belt buckle, boots, and a tee that said Kentucky Honey.

The wind played with the leaves overhead making sleepy sounds. Listening to Brody echoing all the songbirds, Savannah lead the way to an opening in the trees that showed a small cave in the rocks of the hillside. The cave's mouth looked dark against the bright green foliage growing in the sunshine.

"I thought we could stop right up here and have the lunch I packed," she tossed over her shoulder.

"Sounds mighty nice."

"I dearly love this little spot of Heaven on earth."

Savannah was enjoying the best Sunday she'd had in as long as she could remember. Why was Brody so much fun to be around and so easy to cut up with? What had happened to her decision to never get involved again? To be aloof? To never let her heart be hurt again? Gone! Gone with the wind blowing gently through those leaves.

Her heart wanted to spend every minute she could with this man. Maybe she was braver than she gave herself credit for.

Savannah loved spending time with Buttercup, her chestnut horse with the flaxen mane and tail. Buttercup had been picked out by Glenwood and was the most even-tempered little girl around. She was one of the reasons Savannah hadn't left town yet. She could cut a calf from the herd like it was something she was born to do.

Paulo was a gem among horses, too. He would follow Buttercup anywhere. Savannah thought about how easily Brody had won over the big dark bay with his long mane. That horse could read a person's character. He was so smart.

She looked back at the big horse, nearly mahogany in the dappled sun, and smiled at the man on his broad back. Wow, they looked good together.

They slowed in the clearing and stopped to get off the horses. Savannah spread out a gingham tailgating blanket and food and water while Brody tied the horses up nearby.

There were boiled eggs, ham roll-ups, broccoli salad, home-made ranch dressing, and bottled water. It was a small feast.

She looked up as Brody approached and said, "Oh! I forgot dessert! Cookies!" She batted her eyes at him.

He sat down right beside her and started piling the broccoli salad on a paper plate. "Well, this meal is going to spoil me enough. I don't need anything sweet. Look who I'm with. Look where she brought me."

"Why, thank you." She dipped her ham roll-up in ranch dressing and took a huge bite.

"Welcome. Been in that cave?"

"A few times. It's not very big, but it makes this place so pretty." She enjoyed watching him eat his lunch.

"Tell me something about your family that I don't know. I don't really know much at all," Brody said as he started shoveling ham roll-up into his mouth. "Yum. There's smoked Gouda in there!"

Savannah watched him for a moment longer before she answered. She liked that the man had a good appetite. "Well, it's a small family. It's just been me and daddy since I was in middle school, so I chose Lana and her four brothers to be like family. Mom left about then, twice. She's somewhere in Seattle. She said she just had to 'find herself.' She's kind of a hippy and so very calm. Her name is even Skye. I don't think she ever realized that she hurt dad and me both when she left."

"How did you feel about that?" Brody asked.

"I've gotten used to it now. I text with her pretty often. Daddy still loves her and I don't know that he's even looked sideways at another woman since then."

Brody smiled. "Even Ms. Beulah Burton?"

Savannah laughed. "We all know she'd like to get her hooks into my daddy. She's a little too colorful for dad."

Brody took a long pull from the water and said, "Your dad seems ok with his life though; happy, in fact."

Savannah nodded while she pushed her plate away and leaned back on her elbows. "Your turn."

Brody frowned. "My turn, what? Oh, tell you something about my family? Ok, that's fair. My dad and your dad knew each other at UK. They had agriculture classes together."

"Already heard that. Go again." She waited for him to open up to her about his family, even just a little.

"Well... there's just me and my older brother. He's vain and selfish and thinks he is God's gift to women. He also thinks he's smarter than me and loves to point that out. Fun guy to be around. That's part of what helped me decide to come here."

Savannah laughed. "Wow. I'll have to thank him for that someday. Ok, what about your mom?"

Brody grinned. "She's kind of a calm hippy, too. Does yoga and grows organic herbs. She's a good cook. Still with my dad, although they seem to have pretty separate interests, you know?"

"I don't know, not really," Savannah shrugged. "Wanna wade in the creek?" Savannah asked as she pulled her boots and socks off, not waiting for an answer. She rolled up bottoms of her jeans a little and jumped up.

You can lead a horse to water, but you can't make him drink - I'm not agreeing with that old saying today. I'm going to lead a horse to water, and I can make him drink; drink from my kisses!

She suddenly couldn't get Brody's kisses out of her mind. She hoped there wasn't broccoli in her teeth.

She headed toward the cool shallow water running by and choose a place where the banks were low to step in. Only then did she look back at Brody. He was shaking his head and grinning while he pulled his boots off.

"Is it cold?" he asked.

"Come and see."

After rolling up the bottom of his jeans, he splashed into the water near her and gave her a hug. Then he took her hand and started walking carefully upstream.

How far is he going to walk up this creek bed? I can't kiss him until he stops.

She followed him as closely as possible while placing her feet on the slippery rocks. "Hey. Lana and I are going out for a couple of drinks tonight maybe. You want to come? Or meet us there? You could add to your bourbon knowledge."

"Dang. I've got a five A. M. start to my day tomorrow, little darling. I don't think I'd better take you up on that. But, I want you to promise me you two will be careful."

"Promise."

Brody pointed out a big bullfrog just to their left. "Look at that."

"That's some good eating right there. Have you ever frog gigged? Frog legs with gravy and fried eggs? That is something I'm pretty good at." Savannah pushed her bare foot near the frog but it did not move.

Brody shook his head. "No, but you could teach me how to frog gig and how to cook them, too. I'd like that." He turned around and pulled her into his arms, looking up at the sun dancing down through the trees hanging over the edge of the Bourbon Creek. "I'd love to learn things like that from you."

It seemed as though the wood thrushes were singing back and forth in the trees, just for them. They were singing a beautiful song with both echoing and new phrases intertwining like honeysuckle vines.

Savannah loved the feel of this man. She hoped she would always remember this perfect moment, with the warm sun above and the cool water running by their ankles. She put her head against his chest to feel his heartbeat and took a big deep breath. "You do agree that we have a growing desire for each other?" She reached up and felt the scruff along his jawline.

She felt Brody's laugh in his chest. "I certainly do. You know what else? I love how you just say what you think, and don't dance around things. You are a brave woman. Thanks for, hopefully, feeling safe with me."

She looked up into his eyes and reached up on tiptoes to kiss him. Closing her eyes, she felt the longing for him more than ever. She lost herself in the dance of the kiss for several minutes, feelings swirling around them like the leaves being carried downstream around their feet. She kissed him with promises she didn't know she could make this quickly in a new relationship. She kissed him with real love- new and exciting and breathless, love.

Brody was the one who pulled away finally. With a serious look on his face he said, "Wow. Savannah, listen. Don't leave town. Stay here and let's give these feelings we have for each other a real chance. I know you've been hurt, but I don't believe for one minute you really think that casual relationships are ok. I think we may have something really special here between us."

Savannah smiled. "Oh, I bet you say that to all the girls you take to church."

"No, I don't. I don't want you to ever again be a sermon illustration..." Brody gave her a playful look.

She laughed as she reached down and splashed him, then tried to run back down the slippery creek. He caught her as she almost fell into the water.

They took hands again and headed back to the horses, steady on their feet together.

Savannah didn't miss the symbolism of feeling steady when they held hands, and stronger together.

This is how it's supposed to feel when you find the right man.

"So, does this mean we are dating? Scary stuff." she teased. "What if Lana and I both have too much bourbon tonight? Could I call you to come drive us home?"

As Brody reached for their boots he said, "I've got to be able to trust you, little darling. You've got to decide to trust me. That way we can try to build a relationship worth everything. I can promise I will make it worth your while. So, don't be going too crazy with Lana." He gathered up the picnic supplies and took them to the horses who were patiently grazing nearby.

She could feel that he meant every word as he handed her up into the saddle. She still had to ask another question. "You're going to make me wait to get all intimate and frisky, aren't you?"

Brody laid one hand on the mare's neck and one on her leg, as if to settle them both. He looked into her eyes and smiled. "I'm going to try real hard to do just that. I think it's going to be tough to do, but it will please God and we both want Him in our decisions, right? So, don't be too hard on me, pretty girl. Besides, the longer we wait, the more special it's all going to be."

"Oh, my goodness." Savannah could hardly believe how happy her heart was with all of this. "Here I've been trying to convince myself that no-strings relationships are the only way to go. You are not a normal man, Brody Bangfield."

"Thank you very much, Savannah Stetson. I'll take that as a compliment."

"I meant it as one."

They started back to the big barn. Paulo and Buttercup knew the way.

"Our initials are funny, huh? BB and SS."

The slow rocking of the horse beneath her made her sleepy as she listened to the birds call back and forth overhead. Brody whistled back at them now and then, sounding just like them.

She called up to Brody, "Hey! You wanna take a nap in the hammock when we get back?"

"Sunday naps with you? Something I'm looking forward to. I'm going to have to get busy though. You go on home and take a nap."

"Ok. Fine. Just remember this - There are two ways to argue with a country girl, and neither one of them works - at least for long."

Brody was laughing at that as he pulled her down from the horse and up against his body for a drawn out and delicious moment. "I'll take care of the horses, sleepy girl. We'll take a nap together soon enough. You go draw some red hearts in your planner."

She kissed him on the cheek and walked toward the house.

"That's a very good idea!"

CHAPTER 13

*B*rody sat on the back steps of the bunkhouse that
night. He looked up at the clouds moving in from
the west. He held his phone. He had texted Savannah a quick
message. "Thanks for a wonderful day." He wished she would
text him back soon.

He needed to get to bed. He leaned against Cinder, sitting
beside him, and said, "I can see why you like her best. I do, too."
The dog put his paw on Brody's leg while Brody pulled loose fur
out of Cinder's coat.

Her text came in just then. He read Savannah's words.

"Thank you, too! Remember I forgot dessert?"

He texted back, "Are you flirting with me?"

She texted, "Well, yes, of course, but if you want to run up to
the back porch for two minutes, I'll have you a bag of home-
made peanut butter cookies...and a goodnight kiss."

"Goodnight cookie kiss?" he sent back.

Brody grinned as he stood up and looked down at Cinder.
"Want to race me to the back porch? Come on!"

He took off like a shot, with Cinder matching his pace. They
got to the back porch in record time, hardly breathing hard.

Brody gazed at Savannah, still in her jeans and that big belt buckle, but barefoot with her beautiful hair in two braids.

He took the bag of cookies she held out to him.

"You said run up here. I ran. Cinder almost beat me." He put his arms around her and rocked from one foot to the other in a big hug, almost like dancing. "Those cookies look so good. Glad I've got milk."

She rocked back and forth with him. "Well, I've heard that the way to a man's heart is through his stomach. Now, our two minutes is almost up, so kiss me goodnight, ok? I'm trying to be good."

Brody looked her in the eyes and said, "Oh, you are doing a good job of being good, so good you've taken up residence in my head. Most of the time you are all I can think about. That's not something I was expecting."

He kissed her with increasing urgency, trying to keep his wits about him. He never wanted to let her go. He felt her melt against him and press herself exactly into his body as the kiss lengthened and deepened. Oh, she felt so good.

Glenwood came through the darkness and up onto the porch saying, "Hey, kids! What are y'all..?"

Brody and Savannah jumped. They tried to pull apart from the heated embrace but somehow their belt buckles were caught on each other's! They awkwardly shifted, hands working on the metal buckles, faces turning red.

Brody felt the embarrassment crawl up along the back of his neck. He knew exactly how suspicious they must have looked to Glenwood, his new boss. After all his attempts to leave the boss's daughter alone, here he was caught in an embrace that they couldn't get untangled from.

Glenwood cleared his throat just as they finally moved apart. "Didn't mean to bother you. Cinder seemed to want me to come back here..."

Cinder gave a short bark, to agree.

Brody looked at Savannah, his eyes asking what they should say as the silence lengthened.

Savannah turned to face her father. "Daddy, our belt buckles got tangled up when we were kissing each other good night. That's it. We, um, decided we kind of liked each other today, so... there you go." She snapped her fingers twice and smiled.

Glenwood opened his mouth, then closed it again, looking from one to the other.

Brody loved the honest mouth on his boss's daughter. He looked at Glenwood, who was grinning from ear to ear. "I hope that's all right, sir. We are going to take our time getting to know each other better. Well, goodnight, sir. Night, Savannah."

"Well, if that don't beat all. I did tell y'all to have fun after church," Glenwood mumbled.

"Night." Savannah grinned and quickly headed into the house.

Glenwood turned back to Brody. "Should we have a little George T Stagg, to celebrate?"

"Is that the name of another bourbon?"

"Yes. One of the best around."

"I can't keep them all straight yet. Can I get a rain check?" Brody grinned and held up the bag of cookies. "Milk goes better with peanut butter cookies."

CHAPTER 14

Savannah glanced up at the clock and went to lock the door to the bank lobby. She loved when it was just her and Lana doing the 4 to 6pm drive-through-only session. She had lots of things to catch Lana up on and knew that they could easily keep up with the last customers of the day and still talk. Then they would count out their drawers and put them in the safe.

Dealing with counting money used to make her nervous but now she could do it without thinking about it at all. She had even stopped worrying about getting held up by a robber. She prayed it never happened to her.

She thought back to the other night when Brody had told her she had taken up residence in his head. She'd thought he was going to say "taken up residence in my heart." Oh, well, close enough for now. She would work on it, and enjoy the ride.

Waving at the other employees as they left, she did a little line-dance move across the lobby and back down to the drive-through section, weaving in and out of the afternoon sun slanting through the windows

"I'm guessing there's a big reason you are doing all that dancing at work," Lana said. "Spill the details, girl!"

"Well, you are going to just tell me we are moving too fast and that I really don't know Brody nearly enough yet." Savannah danced a little heel-dig with a kick-ball-change before she sat back down on her stool with a flourish.

"No, I'm not. I kind of like him with you. You're happy, right? Because you seem really happy," Lana said.

"How can you tell?" Savannah asked.

"Dancing at work is kind of a clue."

Both of them had to focus on the cars that pulled up just then with after-work transactions. Savannah let her mind wander to the moment Brody's belt buckle was caught on hers, and her dad had come up on them at just that awkward moment.

Lana laughed so hard when Savannah finally got to tell her about that. "I'd like to have seen your dad's face! What did you say?"

"I just went ahead and told him that Brody and I decided we liked each other, a lot," she laughed. "He sure didn't seem to mind."

"I guess not. Oh! Guess what? I have big news, too! Bobby Joe's going to be on the road with work again for a few days and won't be back in time for our tickets to the Country Music Backroad Show."

Savannah looked up. "Oh, no! Think you can sell them?"

Lana shook her head. "I'm not about to sell 'em. You are going to go with me!"

"But isn't it right before our Kentucky Young Farmers Day?" Savannah asked. She didn't think that was going to work at all.

"Yes, the night before. Listen, I have it all figured out. I'll drive. We'll go and not stay over. You can sleep in the car on the way home if you want. I'll come to Young Farmers Day early. Come on, you can do it!" Lana looked so excited.

Savannah thought about it for a minute. She could see how much this meant to Lana. The kid's day plans were in really good shape, there were lots of reliable volunteers, and everything that could be bought ahead was ready to go. "Ok, you convinced me. Girl's trip!"

"Yay! No bourbon. Just great music!"

"We can power through!" Savannah flexed her biceps.

Lana threw her hands up in the air. "Yay! Bobby Joe said you wouldn't leave me hanging." She started counting out her teller drawer, her hands flying through the daily task.

Savannah said, "I'll have to tell Brody. I hope he doesn't turn into one of those possessive men that never want you to spend time with anyone else. I don't want to deal with that even if he is a big ole sexy cowboy."

Lana laughed. "Well, I just hope he doesn't turn into one of those 'Kentucky Derby Man" types."

"Kentucky Derby Man? What is that?" Savannah hadn't heard that one before.

"Oh, you know - The Fastest Two Minutes in...Racing?"

Savannah covered her face with her hands and giggled. "Lana, stop! Oh, my gosh!"

Savannah didn't need any help thinking about that stuff.

CHAPTER 15

*A*fter a hot day of hard work with the herds, Brody buttoned up his red plaid shirt and pulled on a pair of running shoes. He hurried out of the bunkhouse and headed toward Savannah. He was having a quick meal to talk about some more details for the fast-approaching Kentucky Young Farmers Day. .

He had worked so hard from seven in the morning to five-thirty with cattle and the huge red tractor and dust and sweat and good honest work. He wouldn't need another work-out today. It was like he worked out all day already.

Brody smiled up at the sky and thanked the Lord for his ability to do hard work and for his growing attachment to this land and the very special people and animals who lived on it. He felt a real connection to this place and it felt really good. He felt as if he had found his purpose.

He would have to go back out west and visit his dad and mom, maybe around the holidays, but he was feeling at home pretty quick as a cowboy in Kentucky.

Maybe he could bring his own horse back with him then. It

would be a long drive with a horse trailer but Bandit might like Kentucky, too. Glenwood had already given this idea the go-ahead when Brody was hired on.

He had a view of the garden as he came out of the trees along the path to the house. The garden was growing so quickly. It seemed like plants could grow a few inches in a day at this time of year.

He saw Savannah standing just inside the rows of bright green pole beans. She was standing, legs apart, with both hands wrapped around a pistol.

Wait!

Brody began to run.

Bang!

Brody ran even faster, sprinting to reach her as fast as he could.

He pushed her hands down and moved her behind him, all in one movement. He pulled his pistol out of the waistband of his jeans. "Hold still," he said quietly, all his senses on high alert and looking around. Then he saw the pieces of what was left of a large snake.

"Why? You going to shoot that dead copperhead for me?" Savannah asked. Several feet down the row, she pointed to what was left of the copperhead she had just killed. "I should have brought Cinder with me. I know that."

Brody tucked his gun away as he glanced at the dead snake. He put his hands on Savannah's shoulders, searching her eyes just to make sure she was all right. "You? You shot a copper-head? You scared me to death, Savannah Kay Stetson. Wow. Where did you have a gun?"

She pulled up her shirt to show her waist encased in black lace. "In my Belly Band, of course." She grinned at the look on his face. "What did you think was happening when my gun went off?"

"I thought maybe you shot that Handy Haner guy or something!" Brody shrugged.

Savannah laughed out loud as she put her gun away. "Randy Haner. Oh, he needs shooting, but I hope I'm not the one that has to do it."

Brody reached down and gave her a quick kiss. "Well, good to know you can take care of yourself." He actively worked to slow his heart rate down. Between the gun going off and being so close to this amazing little woman - this was not an easy task.

"Thanks for coming to my rescue though, really, even though I didn't exactly need it. Let's go eat."

Brody followed her closely and ran right into her backside when she stopped and turned around. "What?"

"I was going to the garden to snip some fresh lettuce! I forgot."

"I'll get it, ok? You head on up to the house. Your dad might be wondering why a gun went off in his garden."

He sent her toward the main house while wondering if there was much of anything she could not handle.

LATER, while they ate rosemary chicken thighs, a salad, and roasted carrots, Brody heard about Savannah and Lana's upcoming trip to see the Country Music Backroad Show. She seemed excited about it as she named some of the performers. He hadn't heard of most of them, but he loved seeing her so happy about going. He was learning how much she loved music. He would never forget that day in the barn, when he was singing and she jumped right in. All that singing had led to their first kiss and -

"Brody?"

"What? Oh. I was thinking about when the two of us sang in the barn, right before our first kiss. I guess my mind wandered." He gave her his best smile.

"Well, I guess I am rattling on and on about the Backroad Show but it's going to be so perfect! I know we all have everything in good shape for the Young Farmers Day. It is the very next day though.

"I even made a big chart for volunteers to check off the things as they get finished, like moving chairs and tables and decorations. We can handle it. I've helped run it three times already so no worries there, unless it rains. Pray for no rain!"

"I will do that," he said.

"Lana said she would drive us back right after the show. Brody, we won't be drinking any bourbon. I don't want you to worry, ok? Hmm. Maybe one of us could drink a little bourbon and the other one could drive? Hey, you can pick which one drives! Which one?"

He thought her smile could light up a whole town as he said, "Well, which one of you is the better driver?"

"Lana, for sure. You gotta' trust me on that," she said.

"I do trust you, little darling. Where'd you learn to make this rosemary chicken thighs recipe?"

"From the Feeding Ger Sasser food blog. Isn't it delicious?" Savannah reached for a few more carrots. "I have a few more meals tagged there to make for you soon."

"Yum. Good. Listen, you and Lana go have a great time at the Backroads Show. I know it's coming up this weekend. Just text me when you get back, ok? Then I'll be able to sleep better."

"I promise."

He started clearing the table. It was the least he could do after she'd made him a nice dinner while they caught up on things. "And if you do both drink, just let me know where to come get you."

"No worries, BB," she laughed.

He'd never had anyone call him BB before. Maybe one day soon he would tell her his middle name was Boone. She would get a kick out of that.

He watched as she filled a big plastic container with the leftovers. "I'm going to run this meal over to Mizz Myrtle's place. Why don't you go with me?"

Brody's heart filled to overflowing. Here she was taking care of her neighbor, on top of everything else she kept up with. "I'd love to meet her. Your dad has mentioned her a couple of times."

Savannah told him a little about growing up with Mizz Myrtle nearby as she drove them over to the old storybook house deep in the woods.

"I have seen her rip the head off a chicken, and before dinner, you would be drooling in anticipation of eating her chicken and dumplings!"

"That's what I would call fresh chicken," Brody laughed.

"I used to probably drive her crazy in the summers. I always wanted to hang out there. I learned how to cook, how to make Kentucky white oak baskets, and how to quilt and sew, too. But, I don't have the patience for much of that."

"She sounds like a grounding influence on you when you were growing up," Brody said, imagining Savannah trying to sit still long enough to stitch on a quilt.

Mizz Myrtle threw up a gnarled hand when they came around the curve in the gravel road. She was sitting on the porch with an apron over her lap, breaking green beans and putting them into a large pot beside her.

They got out and took the food to her.

"Hey, we had some dinner leftovers, so I thought I would bring them to you. I wanted you to meet Brody, too.

"Brody Bangfield, this is Mizz Myrtle. Brody is daddy's new herdsman and manager."

Savannah sat down at the old woman's feet and began helping her with the green beans.

"Very pleased to meet you," Brody said.

"Thank you. Come on, sit down for a minute. You don't

sound like you're from around here, and I don't recall ever meeting any Bangfields," she said. "Where are your people from?"

Brody explained how he had grown up out west, but was really beginning to see why some people thought Kentucky was a very special place.

He watched Savannah break beans at a very fast pace, so that the older lady wouldn't have to do them after they left.

"I'd get my dulcimer out and we could sing a little, but my hands have been too stiff here lately," she said.

"Oh, that's ok. We don't have time to stay long tonight anyway. But we will have to come back sometime soon and sing with you. Brody's a very fine singer."

Mizz Myrtle leaned back and wiped her hands on her apron. "Oh, I would have guessed that right away. Now, girl, you don't need to be wasting your time with a man that can't sing! Brody, this girl right here? Why, she can sing harmony to any song ever sung, I do believe."

Savannah got up and hugged the dear little old woman and said her goodbyes.

Brody didn't think Savannah had a clue that she had a real gift of making people feel happy and appreciated. She had a good heart, and that made him smile.

She dropped Brody off down at the bunkhouse after a few quick kisses in her car.

"I'm glad you get to go see the live music with Lana this weekend. I'll catch up with a lot of things around here. It's going to be a busy weekend," he said.

"Maybe one of the best weekends ever!"

"Your Backroads Show, the Kentucky Young Farmers Day, and church at Pleasant Hillside. You're going to have to go back to work just to get any rest, Savannah," he said.

"I'm young. I got this!"

"Goodnight, little darling."

"Night. I've got to focus on one event at a time! Lana and I will just sing along at the top of our lungs with singers like Emily Jamison. Brody, it will be a night to remember!"

CHAPTER 16

*S*avannah and Lana had turned a few heads as they climbed the stairs and found their seats at the music venue, and no wonder. Both of them were beautiful girls with shining long hair under straw cowboy hats, snug jeans, and colorful embroidered cowboy boots.

Lana had on a red plaid shirt with fringe along the sleeve seams. Savanna had chosen a reddish brown summer sweater that set off the color of her hair, with suede strips criss-crossing up both sleeves.

They looked good and they knew it.

"Girl, these are great seats. Thanks again." Savannah looked all around. "I love that there's no one in the seats right in front of us either."

"Well, so far," Lana laughed. She settled into her seat. "I'm going to try to just relax until the live music starts. I'll never sit down after that."

Savannah smiled at her oldest friend and thanked her for driving them all this way. Lana had 4 brothers and no sisters, so Savannah had always counted her as 'the sister you get to pick out.'

Savannah said, "Emily Jamison! I didn't think I'd ever get to see her in person! I love her strawberry blond hair. The only thing that could make this any better is if Bobby Joe and Brody could be here with us, like a double date!"

Lana laughed. "Or Chris Stapleton and Willie Nelson. That would be a fun double date, too."

"Pretty sure they are both married, Lana."

"Oh, yeah. We'd better stick with Bobby Joe and Brody then. We could sure do worse than that."

Savannah offered to go get them something to drink or eat, or even see if they were selling tee shirts, but Lana turned it all down.

"You wouldn't let me fill up your gas tank or pay for my ticket, either. Come on!"

Lana gave her a hug. "You are here, and I am here. That's all we need right now. Let's live in the moment and enjoy some fine Kentucky musicians!"

It was almost time for the show to start. The crowd started making some noise as a backstage crew member brought out Emily's Jesse Thomas guitar and placed it in the stand.

The lights suddenly went up onstage and Emily Jamison walked out to the mic in the center of the stage, all long legs, strawberry blonde hair, and a baseball cap. She shot the crowd a big smile as she picked up her guitar and suddenly the whole place was on their feet. You could feel the electricity building and rolling in waves toward the stage.

The bass and drums began laying down the solid backbeat for the guitars to bounce around on.

"I hope she does Bitter & Sweet," Lana shouted near Savannah's ear.

The first few notes told them both that Emily was starting with Purple Cadillac. The crowd knew, too, and everyone started moving to the song as Emily started singing.

Emily had a way of drawing connections to everyone in the

crowd as the stories unfolded in her songs. People sang along to the memorable melodies as she worked through more of her set - A Thing To Lose, a haunting cover of Blue Bayou and then the tune they'd all been waiting for, Bitter & Sweet.

"She can handle this crowd like a real superstar," Savannah said, knowing she sounded like a fan-girl. "We should be glad we caught her act while we could afford it."

Emily looked out at the crowd from center stage and thanked them for letting her share her songs with them, and headed off the stage, dancing in her unique and almost awkward way.

The crowd stayed on their feet and wouldn't stop clapping until she came dancing back out. She picked up her guitar again. "Ok, guys, I guess I'll do one more song. How about "Better Than Me."

Knowing it was the last song of the set made it even more beautiful to the crowd and Savannah knew she would always hold this night in her memories.

"Thanks again, Lana," she said, nudging her dear friend.

"I'm just glad I talked you into being here with me. Don't worry about the kids coming to Farmers Day. We got this!"

Then Lana pointed to the stage where they were setting up for Tim Holmes and the Hired Guns. "Remember when we first downloaded Tim Holmes' Won't Let Go album?"

Savannah shivered. "If I had a dollar for every time I listened to Only Got Tonight and Hold On Baby, we could go on a serious shopping spree at Boot Barn!"

"Hold On Baby. We used to drive around all the horse farm back roads in college, too. Remember?" Lana sighed. "Those were the days."

Savannah giggled. "It wasn't that long ago."

Tim Holmes and the Hired Guns, live on stage, did not disappoint. The group kicked back with Blowin' Outta Town and Bakersfield and building throughout the set to Nothing More and some great Chris Stapleton covers.

Tim ended the night doing one last song without the band. "Oh, he's going to make me cry. He's talking about his sister." Savannah had read stories about how he had lost his sister to cancer. "I don't know how in the world he can sing this song and not get all choked up."

"I'm choking up, for sure," Lana said softly.

Tim Holmes and his Guild acoustic guitar ended the night of music with the tribute song called Pretty Jenny. He stood there alone in his flip flops and shared his heartache with the crowd.

Savannah wasn't the only one who was wiping away tears. It seemed like everyone in the crowd had lost someone to cancer somewhere in their life. Tim Holmes was a tortured creative who knew how to put the pain in a Kentucky song.

It was a bittersweet way to end the evening.

THE HOUSE LIGHTS came up and the canned music started playing Chris Stapleton's Millionaire. The girls gave each other a big hug. They looked around to soak up everything before they started to head to the car for the long drive home.

They gathered up all their things and started stepping sideways in their aisle as other people made it into the stairways.

"Hey, we should go look at the tour shirts before we go. Why not, right?" Savannah said to Lana.

"I thought you'd be raring to get out of here and hurry on home since we have so much to do tomorrow. But, it's ok with me," Lana answered.

"Oh, my gosh, look! What the heck? I thought I saw Brody!" Savannah pointed down and one section over.

"Where? No way. What would he be doing here?" Lana asked while searching the crowd. "I don't see him anywhere."

"Right there, look! Maybe he's surprising me? Or checking

to see if we can drive home all right?" Savannah stretched her long legs. "I think he just saw me. Let's go down and...wait a minute. Who's...he is here with a girl? Son of a biscuit eater..."

"No way! Where?" Lana finally spotted him in the crowd below. "Wow. It does look like him." Her voice faded away.

The swaggering cowboy, with a beautiful redhead, started moving down the stadium stairs, taking the girl's hand and making a way through the crowd. The redhead laid her other hand on his back, following as close to him as possible in the tight crush of the crowd. They looked very comfortable with each other. They exchanged words with their mouths searingly close to each other.

Savannah's heart was absolutely crushed. She couldn't take her eyes off of that distinctive cowboy hat in the crowd. "Come on. Let's follow them," she said through gritted teeth.

Lana hesitated. "Maybe it's his sister."

"He wouldn't be holding his sister's hand like that."

Lana was realizing the same thing. "Hey, Savannah? You aren't going to talk to him, are you?"

"No. Never again," Savannah ground out.

"Ok. Good. That's good."

"No. Nothing is good," Savannah spit out while narrowing her eyes at the back of Brody and the gorgeous redhead.

Savannah sized up the redhead who was wearing a black tank and tight jeans tucked into tall black boots. She disliked her immediately.

The girls moved slowly down the stairs. They followed as closely as they could get but it was nearly impossible to push through the crowd. Everyone was moving towards the exits at the same infuriatingly slow pace.

"Maybe he has a doppelganger?" Lana suggested.

"There's no way! Look at the cowboy hat. Look at that walk! No one walks exactly like that. Oh, he is a snake!" Savannah shouted above the noise all around her. She almost hoped he would hear her.

Part of her wanted to make a scene and let her anger and hurt come roaring out of her pounding heart.

She nearly missed the last step but caught herself.

Keep it together, girl. Getting trampled by the crowd would not help this situation one bit.

When she looked up, Brody and the girl were out of sight. The angry tears in her eyes weren't helping matters either. She couldn't find him and that was probably a good thing.

Country girls know how to handle crap. We've stepped in it, smelled like it, and shoveled it. We will not put up with it!

The crowd was pushing along and Savannah had a moment of ringing in her ears as reality set in.

Brody was a liar, like all the other men. Brody was a liar in the worst possible way and she had fallen for him hard. And, fast. But, here he was with another woman? Why did she jump into love so quickly?

I thought we were a couple! A couple in love, with plans for the future...

Hold your horses, girl. You do not love him yet. NO.

But she knew that she did.

Lana took her arm. "Hey, now! Keep it together. We have to get out of this place before you fall apart, ok?"

"Ok." Savannah wiped the tears from her face. "You're right. Let's go."

Why does nothing ever work out for me? I swear, if I ever look at another man, I'm going to kick myself. Why did I even try?

Savannah didn't buy a shirt on the way out. She didn't remember walking to the parking lot and finding the car. She just followed along behind Lana in a daze while listening to the crazy pounding of her broken heart.

It took a long time for all the cars to get out of the huge

parking lots but Lana took care of all of that, just like she said she would.

Lana was the best friend, ever.

Savannah kept playing the Miley Cyrus song, Nothing Breaks Like a Heart, over and over and over in the car, all the way home.

Lana didn't fuss about it once.

It was the perfect song for an ending to this night.

NOTHING BREAKS LIKE A HEART.

Nothing breaks like a heart.

CHAPTER 17

*I*t was a gorgeous Kentucky farmland Saturday morning. The dew on the grass was chilly and it seemed like the birds were welcoming the promise of a perfect day. Squirrels were skittering across tree branches while the barn cats looked up with no real interest in pursuit.

Brody looked out his kitchen window and washed down the big breakfast burrito with black coffee as fast as he could. Sunrise would be at 7:15 and he hoped to be up at the main house before that. He was ready to help make his first Kentucky Young Farmers Day a rip-roaring success. This day meant a lot to Savannah and her dad.

Besides that, all the kids were coming and they would deserve everyone's best.

He had put in long hours yesterday helping to get everything in place. The tent was ready with tables and chairs, popcorn and cotton candy machines, red flag banners, and watering troughs with canned drinks ready for ice. It sounded like the ice truck was pulling up now for a delivery, right on time.

The high school students from the beta club were going to be running carnival games so they could count the volunteer hours. Their section looked impressive as he walked along. They would also be playing country music through a little sound system. Some of them were already there, yawning and drinking coffee, and cutting up with each other.

He headed to the barns first. Leon and his friends were spreading out hay in the biggest enclosure already. There was a poster board tacked to a support beam with all the animals to be brought into this area. The boys seemed to have everything under control here.

"Morning, fellas. Good to see everyone so busy. Anyone need anything from me right now?" He smiled at them.

"We're good. The tours start around 8:30, after check-in at 8. You'll be back by then, right?" Leon asked with a shy smile.

Brody nodded. "Well before that. I'll bring up a couple of Red Angus calves when I get back."

Leon said, "Bring the cleanest ones, ok? Maybe that one with the white markings on his leg?"

Leon's friend Greg added, "Be sure you mark it off on the poster for Miss Savannah, too, ok?"

Brody left the barn laughing at how that little woman had everyone around here following her planner checklists and posters. She sure did keep things organized.

What a woman!

It was going to be a day to remember.

Leon followed him out.

"Brody, I wanted to let you know I had to go ahead and bring my little brother, Raylee, with me. I haven't seen Mr Stetson yet, to let him know. No one was going to be able to bring him later on, and I didn't want him to miss it. I'll keep that kid busy, don't you worry."

"I'm sure that's fine, Leon. I want to meet him sometime today."

"Ok, thanks." Leon flashed that big smile. "He's filling paper cups with food for feeding the baby goats right now."

"No worries, Leon."

Next Brody headed toward the main house. Maybe Savannah was running around already with her hair all curled and ready to own the day. He figured her mind was going a mile a minute about now. He hoped to be indispensable to her all day long, and hopefully, forever.

He couldn't wait to hear about the music she had heard last night with Lana.

As he neared the big screened-in porch, he glimpsed her sitting in a rocking chair with a quilt around her, holding a huge mug of coffee. Her hair seemed to be up in a messy bun on the very top of her head. She was so beautiful to him, and his heartbeat kicked up a notch.

He lengthened his stride just to get to her sooner.

He thought she looked right at him, but she suddenly jumped up and went into the house, slamming the door behind her.

Well, Brody guessed she wasn't ready yet. Maybe she didn't want him to see her hair in a messy bun on the top of her head. He didn't care though. Heck, he thought it was extremely attractive.

Just as he was about to turn around and go pick out two calves for the petting zoo, Glenwood came out of the house and slowly made his way down the back stairs, holding on tight to the railing.

"Good Morning. You ok there?" Brody asked.

Glenwood rubbed his lower back. "Yes, fine and dandy for an old man, I guess. I'll get the kinks worked out when I get going here. Feels like it's going to rain in these bones of mine."

"Oh, I hope not." Brody looked up at the expanse of clear sky above them.

"Listen, son, I don't know what's up with Savannah this morning, but here's some advice; never corner something meaner than you are." Glenwood shook his head.

"What?"

"She just about took my head off this morning when I poured the last of the coffee. That's not her usual mood in the morning."

Brody appreciated the way Glenwood worded things. That must be where Savannah got it. "I'll give her plenty of space today. Thanks for the warning."

"Surely all the kids here today will cheer her up some! Good grief, she was like some cornered badger in the kitchen."

"Really?"

"Yes." Glenwood smiled as they headed out to the pasture together. He went on. "The neighbor down the road said he would be a little late getting Mizz Myrtle's donkeys up here and he wasn't going to bring his mule after all. I guess we could just let the kids pet Savannah, since she is as stubborn as a mule sometimes."

Brody tried not to laugh at that one.

Savannah probably just hadn't gotten enough sleep. How bad could it be?

He figured she must be tired from the show last night and getting home so late. No wonder she was cranky.

She hadn't even texted him when she got home. He guessed he was going to see a side of Savannah today that he had never seen before.

CHAPTER 18

Savannah ran back up to the safety of her room and texted Lana. "You here yet? Come on up."

"Yes. Parking now," the answer came immediately.

Savannah waited, wondering how in the world she was going to get through this day. Even though she had been up all night and her heart was breaking, she had to do a million things for their regional Kentucky Young Farmers Day, and most of all, for her dad.

That's right, girl. Keep your mind on your daddy. That will help you get through this day. Then you can get the heck out this town, like you've been planning! No time like the present. Men, ugh! Especially a certain one!

"Hey. Seen Brody yet?" Lana burst into the room like a small tornado, ready to beat this day into submission.

"No. Yes. I mean, I did, but I ran back into the house. I don't know if I slept any at all. The last thing I want to do is go greet the kids as they arrive." Savannah laid her head against the window and sighed. "I go from sad to angry, to zoned out, to sad again. It's exhausting."

"We can do it. I'll try to run interference for you when I can," Lana said while picking clothes up off the floor.

"Thanks, Lana. You are the best."

"What are you going to do?"

Savannah squared her shoulders. "I'm going to smile at the children and not let the Young Farmers down. This is too important to Daddy.

"I'm not going to worry about impressing anyone or the fact that my hair looks awful."

Lana agreed. "Atta' girl. 'A messy bun means we're gettin' stuff done.' But, what about after today?"

Savannah hated to say the words to Lana but there was no getting around it.

"I'm leaving. I was planning to anyway, right? I guess I'll head to Lexington or Louisville. I can't be around him. I feel so stupid." She nearly crumbled onto her friend's shoulder.

"It's ok. It's going to be ok," Lana whispered as she hugged her for a minute.

Savannah knew that was the last thing Lana wanted to hear but she just couldn't help it. She was never going to look at another man as long as she lived. Little Miss Independent would be her name, all right. She would love dogs and children and bourbon and her daddy!

Brody had completely pulled her in, hook, line, and sinker. He had said all the right words, made her feel special, and listened to her. He seemed to be too good to be true, and that was exactly what he was. If only she could stop all the memories, like how he had put his body in front of her when she had shot the copperhead in the garden, or how he pressed his body against hers when he helped her off of Buttercup after their picnic down by the creek.

Stop it! Dry your eyes and go get the job done.

She headed out the door toward the big happy day that would no longer be a big happy day.

·   ·   ·

SHE STAYED busy through all the check-in duties. There was a large crowd, probably the biggest ever but that wasn't as exciting as it would have been before last night.

She hardly even noticed how good everything looked. The colorful crepe paper streamers almost annoyed her.

All the people looked so happy, too. Well, she wasn't happy but she wasn't going to let on to anyone about that.

She saw Brody walk by a couple of times but always turned away and kept busy, wishing her heart would stop pounding out of her chest. More than once she overheard other women pointing him out and talking about how gorgeous he was, or how they had seen him around town the last few weeks.

Wow, it was going to be a long day.

Stay busy. Talk to all the kids. Make them smile.

SHE WAS WALKING behind the blackberry bushes when she heard Brody's voice. She couldn't stop herself from listening as he talked to a little boy all decked out in cowboy gear. He couldn't see her from here, so no one would know she was listening.

"Howdy to you, too, little guy," Brody said to a young boy.

"So, pardner, you keeping them doggies in line around here?" the young voice said.

"Well, they keep me plenty busy, but I guess I'm doing ok." She could hear the smile in Brody's voice.

"So, how am I doing?"

"How are you doing what?" Brody asked the boy.

"How am I doing playing this role?" Savannah peeked through the bushes and saw the little boy wink at Brody.

"Role?" Brody asked.

"Yes" The little fellow put his fingers in the belt-loops of his jeans and set one foot up on a rock. "I'm a young and lovable cowboy-to-be, learning from the best! Isn't that YOU?"

Brody seemed perplexed. "What do you mean, exactly?"

"Well, I am pretty sure you are my target. I've been pretending all day that the cameras are rolling!" He nodded.

"Oh, I see. Are you having fun in this role?"

"Yes, but this cowboy costume is hot. On the other hand, there's no lines to memorize, and this Beulah Burton lady pays really well. My mom was tickled to death!"

"Well, that's good," Brody said but he was confused, especially about being the target.

"My mom needs that money. We just moved here this summer and she works for Ms. Beulah at the diner, but she said she didn't know how long she was going to be able to put up with her as a boss-lady.

"Anyway, I'm here so Miss Annabelle Burton can be here, too.

"Oh, and I'm supposed to tell you how wonderful she is, but I don't really know her," the boy shared. Looking around, he put his finger to his lips. "Shhh."

"Hmmm. Well, that's interesting. Have you had plenty of cotton candy and pony rides?" Brody asked. He was starting to understand what the boy was talking about.

"I guess so."

Brody seemed to study the honest little boy a moment.

Savannah was afraid to move, or hardly breathe. She didn't want him to see her eavesdropping.

"Well, that's good, too. So, how can I make today even better for you?" Brody asked.

"Oh, I know! How about a photo with your horse? On your horse? Or feeding and brushing your horse? I have my phone and those photos would look good on my Instagram!"

"Sure thing, little fellow. Let's go."

"Wow, mister! Really? You really are the best!"

"Thanks, little buddy."

"You going to tell them I did a good job with this character I'm playing?"

"You bet." Brody swung the boy up onto his back and galloped toward the barn.

Savannah watched them until they were out of sight.

It was like Brody was two different people. One of them pulled her heartstrings like the best fiddle player in the history of earth, ever. The other one was a womanizer who might very well be the best liar in the history of earth, ever!

She couldn't even remember what she was going to check on next, so she decided to try to mingle with the people working the pony rides until it came to her.

If she worked as hard as she could all day, she would surely be tired enough to get some sleep tonight. She couldn't think of any other way to turn her brain off, or to ease her aching heart.

MUCH LATER, she was carrying another case of bottled water over to the tent when Brody sauntered up in front of her and tried to carry it for her.

Ugh! Why does he have to walk like that? Doesn't he realize his appeal?

Don't cry. Don't cry.

"I'm good." she said and she kept walking, looking straight ahead.

"I'm just trying to help. I'm really enjoying watching the kids with the petting zoo and teaching them about taking care of baby animals. I've hardly had a chance to talk to you at all today though," he said, falling in line beside her. "I like explaining about how we don't use antibiotics or hormones with the cattle here when homeopathic remedies will usually do the trick."

She remained silent.

"Savannah. Talk to me. How can I help you? I have a few minutes before the next tour in the barn."

She ground out, "Ask Daddy."

She had reached the watering troughs and started slamming bottled waters down into the ice, and refused to look up at him. *Stupid gorgeous man, acting like everything was ok! That's not going to do him a bit of good!*

A part of her wanted to hurl the water bottles at his head.

Brody backed up. "Ok. Will you talk to me at lunch?"

"Why? So you can lie some more?" She shook the icy water off her hands and stomped away, determined not to cry, not to yell at him about seeing him at the Kentucky Backroads show, and not to hurt for him any more.

She saw her daddy working the cotton candy machine, laughing with all the families and friends. He was in his element, sharing the farm life with everyone who came out today and making the biggest pink cotton candy she had ever seen.

She took a deep breath and started to go give him a big hug. She'd be darned if she would give him reason to worry about her today of all days!

Wait a minute. I just told Brody to ask daddy about what he could help with next. I'll hunt down Lana over at the hayride first.

ON THE WAY she noticed Annabelle and Beulah Burton trying to walk across the grass. They were holding on to each other and to their snow cones. They both had on high heels that were sinking into the ground with each step.

The impracticality of the Burton women always lightened Savannah's mood, along with the height of Beulah's stiffly hair-sprayed bouffant.

Beulah waved. "Well, hello, Savannah. You must be working yourself to death today. Why, look at your hair," the older woman said, shaking her head.

Savannah smiled in spite of the snarky comment and resisted the urge to reach up and touch her hair. "I sure am. Why in the world are you two here, in high heels? I mean, it's ok, but you don't have kids."

Annabelle's many bracelets clanked as she shrugged. "Why, mother wanted me to meet your father's new employee. She met him at church and couldn't stop talking about how handsome he was."

"Oh, How nice," Savannah lied.

Beulah spoke up. "We know it's Kid's Day. So, I borrowed Annabelle a kid."

Savannah looked at her and said, "Really? Well, where is he?"

"Oh, he's running around here somewhere," Annabelle said as she reached the picnic tables and sat down. "He'll be fine."

Beulah began her usual litany of ways to make everything more to her liking. "Now, Savannah, it is a hot day. Maybe next year you all should think about air conditioning the tents. Valet parking might be helpful also. Be sure and tell your father these ideas came from me. Of course, I'll tell him when I see him, too."

"Ok, then. Y'all have fun," Savannah said over her shoulder as she hurried away. She could hear Beulah's voice for a long time, fussing over Annabelle's choice of a blue snow cone, and what if she had blue teeth when they finally got to talk to Brody Bangfield.

Ugh! They can have him!

THE REST of the day was just a never-ending blur of pain and dread. The misery was getting heavy to carry so she tried to think of any little thing that might cheer her up for a few minutes. She knew that the petting zoo might do the trick, if Brody wasn't in there. It wasn't long before she found her chance.

She forced herself to smile and interact with all the children in the petting zoo when she saw Brody take off in the other direction.

Rabbits, goats, and ponies cheered her up a little. Their earthy smells and soft fur touched her deeply. There wasn't anything on God's green earth much sweeter than little baby animal faces with those big vulnerable eyes.

She watched as Raylee, Leon's little brother, handed out paper containers of rabbit food and showed the other children how to hold their hand flat.

"It might tickle a little," he told all the smaller children gathered around him.

He seemed as sweet as his big brother, Leon. That made Savannah's heart smile for a moment. She didn't know a lot of details but she'd heard they didn't have the best home life.

Maybe Raylee will be one of dad's Young Farmer helpers on Thursdays when he's a little older. He seems like a leader already, like his brother. Wait...I won't be here to see that.

Come on, girl. As Daddy says, when you feel sorry for yourself, go do something for someone else.

She threw herself back into the joys of the petting zoo and families and lots of little children.

Later, she found herself holding someone's slobbering twin babies while the parents fed the goats with their toddler. One baby's onesie said MOMMY'S LITTLE COWBOY and the other said DADDY'S LITTLE COWGIRL.

I can't imagine having two babies at once. They must be teething. They sure are the cutest things around here today.

The babies' brother, the toddler, squealed in happiness when the animals ate from his little outstretched hand. He tried to jump like the baby goats. He laid his head against one of the calves and sighed in happiness.

He deserved a few minutes of his parent's attention so Savannah kept bouncing the twins on her hips. She had a way with babies and used to think she would want to have two or three of her own. *That's not going to happen at the rate I'm going. But, look at these round sweet babies. Aren't they just beautiful? I can see how women get baby fever.*

She hummed and bounced and made faces at the babies.

She overheard several moms talking about that "eye-candy cowboy named Brody and did anyone know his status?"

"I didn't see a ring on his finger."

"Well, he is the finest looking thing I've ever seen!"

"Girl, you are preaching to the choir!"

"I'm fixing to see if he could give my kids some private lessons."

"In what?"

"Well, who cares, really?"

The other moms laughed and giggled about that and said maybe having some private lessons of their own would be fun, too.

Savannah had heard more than enough.

They can all drool over the new Kentucky cowboy now. They can flirt and long for his love! They can have him and his lies! They don't have a clue! Being handsome wasn't enough to make a good life with someone!

She handed the babies back and rubbed the toddler's curly head of golden hair. Then she marched out of the big barn with her head held high, messy bun falling sideways.

SHE HEADED to the picnic tables where the speeches were being practiced. This would be a safer place for her, she hoped.

She could hear laughter from there. It seemed like everyone was having a great time today except her.

Clouds were floating across the blue sky and the leaves on the trees were starting to turn over from a sudden breeze. She wondered if rain was on the way. She could almost smell it.

"Hey, Miss Savannah, ready to hear my speech? I've been practicing in the mirror at home, like you said," one of the teenage girls called.

Savannah sat down among the older kids. "Oh, that's good. I'm ready."

She needed to get off her feet for a few minutes anyway.

She tried hard to pay attention but it was no use. She could only get through a couple of teenagers practicing their speeches for the Kentucky Young Farmers college scholarship. Most years she really dug in to help them polish their performances, but today all the talk of "Master Herdsmen," "sustainable gardening for harvesting," and "antibiotics used on cattle only as a last resort" made her head hurt.

So, she begged off and left them at the picnic tables in very capable hands.

She leaned over and promised Leon she would come back for his practice speech in a little while.

"Beulah Burton better get her big hairdo under cover!" Leon said while looking up at the sky.

Lightening crawled across the sky and thunder rumbled.

She just couldn't be still so she got up to hurry off toward the house when it started raining hard.

The rain came down fast and furious. Everyone grabbed up things and ran for cover, in one direction or another.

The wind kicked up all at once and made the rain seem like it came down almost sideways. Plates and tablecloths blew off the tables in a hectic mess.

Savannah headed for the barn, then thought Brody might be there so she turned right around and headed for the overhang by the silo. Running even though she was already soaked from the downpour, she skidded to a halt in the shadows of the silo where it had a small space out of the pouring rain.

Why did it have to rain, too? It's raining in my heart already. Could this day get any worse?

There stood Brody. He had taken shelter in the same place.

Yes, it could get worse all right! Could he look any more rugged and handsome?

She looked down.

Oh, no. Don't talk to me. Don't get close to me.

Brody took a halting step toward her in the small space. "Savannah, can't you even look at me? What have I -"

"You don't want to look at ME! You want to look at some... some redhead!"

"What redhead? There's no redhead." He looked at her like she had lost her mind.

Silence.

"Where is that coming from? Talk to me." Brody pleaded gently, as if she were some cornered wild animal.

"I am NOT talking to you!" Savannah shouted and turned away so she wouldn't watch the raindrops dripping off his cowboy hat. "How could I have ever been so stupid?"

Just then Leon skidded out of the rain and right in between them. "Wow, where did this crazy storm come from?" he said.

"I sure didn't see it coming," Brody said, still looking at Savannah, who didn't miss his double meaning.

She was glad her face was wet from the rain so her fresh tears wouldn't be noticeable. Part of her wanted to hit him. Part of her wanted to kiss him, hard.

She knew that focusing on the kids at the Farmers Day event was her only hope of getting through the rest of this day. "Hey, Leon, as soon as it lets up a little, let's run to the barn! Like, NOW!"

Not giving Brody a second look, she took off in the rain,

which hadn't lessened up in the least. She dodged the straggling crepe paper streamers bleeding into the wet surfaces of the regional Young Farmers Day.

Leon ran right behind her.

Brody watched them go through the water pouring off the overhang, knowing there was a terrible misunderstanding somehow, but not knowing what it was or how to fix it.

CHAPTER 19

*A*fter the storm passed on overhead, the day was winding down. Most of the crowd was going home and Brody worked hard to help everyone get the event cleaned up. He picked up the wet decorations with Leon and his friends, and made sure all the petting zoo animals were back where they belonged. He also checked on the Beta Club kids. Many hands were making short work of the clean-up.

He knew staying busy was the best way to not worry about Savannah. She sure had a bee in her bonnet, as Glenwood would say.

Glenwood walked up just then, limping more than usual. Brody opened a folding chair from the stack beside him and put it beside Glenwood. "Sit down right here and take a load off. You've done the work of three men today."

"Don't mind if I do, son." He wiped off the seat with his handkerchief and eased himself down into the chair.

"I just wanted to say I'm proud to be a part of all this," Brody said. "It's an honorable thing to do, providing so much fun for a free event."

Glenwood eased himself onto the chair. "Well, thank you.

Oh, ow. I might have picked up too many sticky toddlers today. They all seemed to want to sit on a pony and I can't blame them. I'm going to sleep like a rock tonight. I may need to do some of those crazy kettlebell workouts with you before I get some grandbabies of my own."

"Any time, sir. I'd really like that."

Glenwood chuckled. "Helping me with grandbabies, or helping me with kettlebells?"

Brody shifted his weight from one foot to the other. "Kettlebells, sir."

"You think it would do me good?"

Brody was sure of it. "If you start out carefully, you could build your fitness a lot. I could show you photos of guys older than you doing all kinds of pull-ups and rope climbs and stuff."

"Ok, I'm going to sleep on that," Glenwood said.

Brody hoped he really would consider the help, as he turned back to the work.

Although worried sick about Savannah's change in her attitude toward him, Brody was feeling good about the outcome of the big day. He was stacking the chairs and tables up into a truck with a few of the younger boys so they could drive them back to the Pleasant Hillside Baptist Church fellowship hall.

Glenwood rubbed his shoulder absentmindedly and said, "Now, Brody, after you run these chairs back, you call it a day. We're just about put back together here. Well, we do have two cars stuck in the mud down near the turn-off." He grinned. "A couple of certain ladies parked where they weren't supposed to in the first place. That rain really made a mess of it, but Bobby Joe is working on getting them out. Did you see that?"

"No, sir. You sure he doesn't need me?"

"Nah. He's got a hidden winch mount on his Ford. I told him not to throw too much mud on those ladies!" Glenwood chuckled. "Two tiny little cars belonged to Beulah Burton and her daughter Annabelle. Both of those cars are stuck! Don't that beat all?"

Brody said, "I guess the apple doesn't fall far from the tree."

"Beulah was told by more than one person that parking there was a bad idea. Of course, nobody can tell her anything. Funny part was Beulah had talked Annabelle into pushing her car and when that woman gave it the gas, she threw mud all over her daughter, head to toe. Now, who would ever think Annabelle could push a car in those fancy high heels she wore here anyway? All Beulah did was just to dig her car in further, too."

"Did they have that cute little boy with them?"

Glenwood nodded. "I asked Beulah why they were at our Young Farmers Day in the first place since they didn't have kids. Annabelle actually said her mom borrowed her one so she could meet the 'prize-catch' new cowboy."

Brody shook his head. "That's just not normal, although I talked to the little kid and he seemed like an all right sort. I don't think they borrowed him though. I'm pretty sure they hired him. Crazy, huh?"

"Well, I'm glad they are paying him for his time, but it's like those women are all a bunch of hens and you are the new rooster," Glenwood went on as if he didn't even hear Brody trying to change the subject.

"No, sir! I don't want to be a rooster," Brody said.

"I'm teasing you, son. But there's no telling what Beulah Burton would do. She used to come up with all kinds of crazy things to try to get my attention. Oh, the stories I could tell you! She finally did give up, I guess. It took her years to figure out that dog won't hunt, if you know what I mean. Anyway, you sure do seem awful worried about something."

Brody hesitated, then turned back to Glenwood. "I didn't get to talk to Savannah much today."

"There's always tomorrow," Glenwood advised.

"I did see her making kids smile over and over. I even saw her bouncing a baby on each hip in the big barn. Twins. What a sight that was. You raised her right, sir."

Glenwood shook his head. "The Lord knows I tried. Sometimes it still feels like I've had Jesus on speed-dial. He's heard from me about her so much through the years. Now, listen, I don't know why she is mad at you, but she sure enough is."

Brody shoved up the tailgate on the truck. "Well, I don't know why she is mad at me, either. She acted like she couldn't get away from me fast enough all day long. I tried to give her space. I tried to help her. I don't know what else to try, but I sure hope things settle down."

"Maybe I can talk to her later and see what's on her mind," Glenwood offered.

"I'd sure appreciate that," Brody said. "I didn't come here looking for any kind of relationship, sir. It seems like I've gotten used to being alone the last few years. Women are a lot of trouble, generally. It feels like all women leave eventually, but Savannah? She is something really special."

"That she is."

Brody jumped up into the truck. "She puts my mind on trying to win her over."

"You never know what the future holds, Brody. You seem like the kind of man that wants to fix everything right now, but I guess maybe... just give her some more time to calm down."

CHAPTER 20

Savannah banged two big suitcases down the stairs, knocking into the walls and bruising her legs as she went. She'd be danged if she was going to make two trips. It was like carrying in the grocery bags from the car; one trip, no matter how hard it was.

She rolled the suitcases to the front door. They looked forlorn somehow, as if they knew there was not an adventure or vacation in their future. The purse and a big bag sat there, too.

That was about all she was taking right now.

She had been saving some money, putting back a little out of every paycheck since early in the spring. She still had the money from when she sold her tee shirt screen printing supplies last winter, too.

She walked back to the breakfast nook and pulled a page out of her journal. She quickly wrote a letter to her father.

Dear Daddy,

I'm heading out this morning.

I've been talking about leaving for long enough. I don't have an apartment yet but I've booked a little vacation rental for two weeks just outside of Lexington. I think I will like the area, and it's not too far from you, so don't worry, ok?

I need to do some serious thinking. I fear that I got too close to Brody too fast. (not that close!)

Now, I need to protect my heart. I just can't deal with being around him right now.

He's a great asset around the farm though. You know that, so don't fire him or anything on my account, ok?

I just don't want to get hurt anymore.

I'll call you on Tuesday.

Love you bunches,

Savannah

She shoved back the chair from the table and blew her nose on a paper towel. One more trip upstairs for her pillow and she would be ready to take this trip. She could get more things when she came home for a visit.

She would start a list in her planner.

She could call Mr Quibbley, at the bank, first thing in the morning, and maybe he would just call it a vacation for a couple of weeks, to see how she liked it. He would probably hire her again if she needed that job back anyway.

After she grabbed her pillow, she stood in the living room and looked around at the furniture and the old mirror on the wall.

She wished she were getting ready to go to church with Brody again. She would wear a black and white dress and her black snip toe cowboy boots with the glitter inlay. She would take notes in her Faith planner and thank God for the beautiful summer day. Then they could ride the horses again and have another picnic. They could talk about their families and the feelings they were building for each other.

Brody could echo the sweet high-pitched warblings of the male goldfinches in the trees and she could admire how safe she felt with him.

There had been such real closeness between them ever since the picnic, or at least she thought so.

She shook her head and tried to clear it from thoughts of all she was leaving behind.

Boyfriends always hurt you, lie, and let you down. Just face it.

She hoped she never forgot that again.

She wished she had never gone to the Country Music Backroads Show. That's when her world turned upside down. Brody had ruined everything.

Putting the bags on her shoulder and grabbing the suitcases, she went out the door and headed to her car, banging down the steps. She sat everything down near the trunk of her Honda.

Of course it sounds like all one hundred species of songbirds in Kentucky are singing back and forth this morning. They sound happier than pigs in mud. Well, it must be nice.

She was not going to go anywhere on this farm near Brody, so she couldn't exactly take the chance of going down to the big barn to say goodbye to her little chestnut mare.

"Buttercup, I'm so sorry. I can't say goodbye right now, my heart just couldn't take it," she said aloud. "I guess it's only fair, since I'm not saying goodbye to Daddy in person either. I am such a chicken."

She did whistle for Cinder though. He deserved a big hug, and Savannah knew she needed a hug, too. She wanted to sink her fingers deep into his fluffy black underfur one more time, if he was close by.

He came bounding across the lower fields, tongue out and moving fast.

"Hey, big boy! How's the good boy?" She put a knee on the ground and put her arms around the beautiful black dog. "I wish I could just take you with me, pretty boy."

She laid her head against his shoulder and immediately the tears came again.

"Savannah, what are you doing?"

Brody was standing right there in the shade of the trees, looking all trustworthy and handsome and strong.

Savannah's heart nearly stopped.

Brody! I didn't even hear him walk up. Be calm. Guard your heart.

She sniffled and stood up, shaking her head. She turned toward her car to wipe the tears away and opened the driver side door. "I'm putting things in my car."

"Savannah, it's like you can't get away from me fast enough. Why?" He moved closer. "Please. Tell me why."

She sighed in frustration. Not turning toward him, she said, "I should have known not to get close to you so fast."

Brody put his hand on the car door and she finally looked at him. "I haven't done anything to break your trust in me," he said.

"Wow. That seemed so real. Good job, Brody."

Cinder pushed his way between them, touching them both, as if trying to help keep a connection.

They both reached down to pet the dog and their hands touched. It was like fire through Savannah's veins and she pulled her hand back like it had physically hurt her.

"How could you treat me like that? You know what I'd been through!" she yelled.

"I don't know what you mean. What does that even mean?" he asked.

Cinder put his front paws into the driver's seat and she put her head against his for a hug. That dog! It was easy to see he was trying to distract her from her mounting anger and sarcasm. She could hear him softly whine.

Brody said, "I don't understand why you've got your mind made up to go now, all at once. Can we talk about it later?"

"I don't know."

"Do you need me to carry anything for you? Or, do anything to help?"

"Make sure Buttercup gets lots of love and ride her some. Thanks."

"I sure will. I'll keep an eye on your dad, too. Pop the trunk."

That nearly broke her heart all over again. She let herself have one more selfish moment before she moved the dog from the car.

The silence was suddenly filled with the rhythmic sounds of a woodpecker tapping noisily above them, like a crazy bongo-drummer, with his chisel-like beak. It felt like that red-headed bird was tapping on her heart, and it hurt.

Woodpeckers are redheads! Ugh!

She popped the trunk latch and Brody piled in all her things, then shut the trunk with finality.

"Cinder, down. Good boy. Stay here," Savannah managed to say.

She slid into the car and buckled up while Brody shut her door, like a gentleman.

As she pulled away slowly, she looked into her rear view mirror to see Cinder and Brody watching her, side by side.

She couldn't be sure, but that Kentucky cowboy looked like he was brushing away tears as she drove away.

CHAPTER 21

$\mathcal{J}$t seemed to Brody that the songbirds had been singing sad songs for over a week now. Brody never seemed to want to echo their whistling these days. He knew male songbirds would sing to attract a mate but it made him sad to think about that.

The morning sounds of woodpeckers tapping noisily on tree trunks made it even worse, reminding him of when Savannah had driven away.

He had some errands to run today. Hopefully that would make the hours go fast. First stop was the feed supply store. Glenwood had given him a laminated list decorated with stickers of cows and horses. Savannah surely must have made the list. Reminders of her jumped out at him everywhere he looked.

Brody headed into the store, determined not to talk to her in his head. He would talk to himself.

Feed supply stores all smell the same, no matter what state you are in. It's almost patriotic, to me. American farms and ranches are solidly connected to places like this and they're always full of good people mostly.

See? So far, so good. No longing for Savannah.

I hear little peeping sounds. Might as well head in that direction, even though I don't need any chicks or ducklings.

He walked by the live baby chicks and wondered what Glenwood would think about building a safe place for some chickens.

Chickens wouldn't be a whole lot of extra work and they all ate a lot of eggs. He made a mental note to check on that later.

Fresh eggs made him think of Savannah and how if she were still here he could gather them for her to cook with. She could make things like over easy eggs and deviled eggs. She could use a lot of them when she would make some of her cookies. She just whipped them up like it was no big deal. Chocolate chip. Peanut butter. Oatmeal raisin.

I don't need to be raising chickens with Savannah gone. Maybe she will come back soon though and I'd have this as a surprise for her.

What am I going to do? I miss her so bad I can hardly stand it.

Is she ok? Is she happy? Does she think about me? I can't stop thinking about her.

Savannah, please come home soon.

A COMMUNITY BULLETIN board on the back wall caught his attention. It had photos of local animals for sale or to give away. Right in the middle was a photo of four puppies that looked like some kind of German Shepherd mix. Someone named Malachi Ford was looking for good homes, and they were free.

They had happy faces in black and tan. They all looked so alert and one of them had one ear up and one still flopping over.

On a whim, he tore the phone number off and stuffed it in his pocket.

Malachi Ford. Wonder if he's kin to Lana Ford? Maybe what I need is a puppy to take my mind off things. Cinder would love to have a sidekick. Yeah, that would cheer us both up. The address isn't too far from the Stetson's either.

He saw someone step right in front of him, blocking the aisle.

"I know you," said a guy. He was shorter than Brody and had on a shirt that said "I AM THE MAN."

Brody thought the voice sounded confrontational. "I don't think I know you," he said calmly. He held his ground but was wary and on alert.

"Oh, yeah? You're that cowboy from way out west that came to this part of Kentucky, right? You're trying to push your way into Savannah Stetson's life," said a sarcastic voice. "I don't like that one little bit." This angry little man got a tiny bit closer on each of the last three words.

Brody looked at the guy with the John Deere cap on his head and realized it was Randy Haner. "I don't think we've officially met. I'm Brody Bangfield." He put his hand out but Randy didn't seem to want to shake hands. Brody went on with a sly smile. "So, I do know you, too. You're that Sandy Haner."

"NO." Randy Haner looked like he could bite a nail in two.

"Handy Haner?" Brody asked innocently.

"It's Randy Haner. Randy, with an R. Now, listen here, where is Savannah? She's not at the bank anymore. No one there would tell me anything." Randy was trying so hard to look intimidating. "And, I can't just drive out there and ask Mr Stetson."

"Why not?" asked Brody.

"Why, he's crazy enough to shoot me. So, why don't you just tell me where she is?" Randy looked like he was about to stomp his foot.

Brody sighed. "The way I see it, if Savannah wanted you to know where she was, she would tell you herself."

Brody wasn't about to tell this clown that he didn't exactly know where she was, either.

Randy's face was turning a deep shade of red. "You need to do the right thing and back off. I plan for us to work things out and get back together, so I can be the spiritual leader in our future home!" Randy raised his voice as he lost his temper.

He waited a moment to see if Brody would say anything else. Brody remained silent and calm.

Then Randy Haner kicked a stack of dog food bags twice with his pointy cowboy boots and stomped away while dog food pooled on the floor from a small hole.

Brody watched the angry little man go. He was glad for the silence as he turned back to the items needed for the animals at Stetson Farm. He worked to bring his heart-rate down as he made his way through the list, rubbing the cow stickers with his thumb as if it might bring him luck.

Savannah, dang it all to heck, I miss your bright eyes. I wish you weren't mad at me. I've got to figure this out.

Maybe I need to go to the bank next and see if Lana's working. I do have a check to cash. I wonder if she's mad at me, too.

Before he left, he quickly gathered up a dog leash, food and water bowls, and a bag of puppy food before he changed his mind. It didn't cost much, and he would be prepared, just in case he brought a puppy home anytime soon.

Home. I'm already calling the Stetson place on Bourbon Creek home.

Home is where the heart is, except a piece wasn't there.

BRODY GESTURED FOR AN OLDER LADY, dressed head to toe in University of Kentucky blue gear, to go ahead of him in the bank lobby. It never cost anything to be polite to your elders, but another reason was so that he could be next in Lana's line.

The elderly lady turned around and smiled up at him. "Why,

thank you, son. I always notice and appreciate when a man is polite to me. You have yourself a nice day."

"Yes, ma'am, and you, too. I like your UK outfit."

"Oh! Thank you. I think it helps the team, even when they aren't in season."

"I'm sure it does. Fans make all the difference."

"No fan like a UK fan!"

Lana had caught Brody's eye when he came in the door. That was encouraging. Maybe she wasn't as mad at him as Savannah was.

"Hello, Brody. I thought I might be seeing you in here sometime soon. Can I help you?"

"Well, let's see." He counted things off on his fingers. "You could help get Savannah to talk to me. You can tell me what's got a kink in her chain. You can get her to come home," he said, then signed his name on the back of the check. "You can also put this in my checking account, except for $70 cash."

"Got it."

"Thanks, Lana. Also, you can tell me if you know a guy named Malachi Ford. He has puppies to give away."

"Oh, that's my brother. Small world, huh? Those puppies are cute as a button. But, listen, about Savannah. She made me promise not to talk about how she thought she was falling in love with you, but then... she saw you... somewhere..."

Brody shook his head. "After you two went to the Backroad Show? She was like a different person right after that. How can I fix it?"

Lana was looking at him funny. "Brody, let me ask you something. Did you enjoy the show?"

"What are you talking about? I wasn't at the show. I worked late with Glenwood. Then I did a workout. Then I went to bed with my Kindle." He didn't know where she was going with this.

"You went to bed with your Kindle? Who is Kendall?" she asked, frowning. "Is she a redhead?"

"Haha. Kindle e-reader. I read on all the platforms."

"Truth?" she asked. Her eyebrows seemed to be up as far as they could go.

"Truth," he answered. "She won't answer my texts. I've left four messages for her to please call me back. It's all I can think about."

"Ok, I'll try to talk to her about this," Lana offered. "She's not talking to me as much as usual right now. I'll let you know when she's coming back for a visit, ok? That's all I can do. She needs to be the one to talk to you."

"Thank you so much," Brody said as he folded his cash and stuck it in his back pocket.

"Brody?"

He turned back to her. "Yeah?"

"Get the puppy. They are the cutest things you've ever seen."

"I'm going to go look at them. Did Savannah quit her job here?"

"She took a leave of absence. Mr. Quibbley is so crazy about her, he would give her the job back anytime. He would probably give her anything she asked for."

"Ok, we'll talk soon."

A leave of absence sounds better than quitting. I'm holding on to hope!

He walked across the bank lobby and held the door open for the sweet older lady as she was leaving. He just couldn't give up hope. He just couldn't.

"How about them Cats?" he said, mimicking almost every UK fan in this area of the state.

The older lady smiled back at the cowboy. "All the way, baby, all the way!"

As BRODY WALKED BACK to his truck he realized his stomach was growling. He headed over to the CowTown diner to grab a quick meal to go. He had almost forgotten to eat a few times this week already. Sadness was hard on a body with so much work to do.

No doubt about it, this place knew how to make the most of good cuts of beef, but the parking lot wasn't full. He was glad it was late in the day to be getting lunch. He would be able to park the truck where he could keep an eye on the supplies in the truck bed.

He easily found a seat at the bar as his eyes adjusted to the dim lighting. He eased onto the barstool and pulled out his phone to check the weather for the rest of the week. There were lots of things coming up at the farm that would be easier if it wasn't going to rain too much.

He needed to move the bull, Bruno, to a different pasture and he wasn't looking forward to that. He was also coming up on a deadline for a national article about sustainable remedies with sick cows to reduce antibiotic use. The fence line they shared with Mizz Myrtle's property line was going to need attention before anything else. There was a lot to keep up with.

Maybe I need a planner, like Savannah. I wish I could ask her which one would be good for me - smaller, bendable for a back pocket, and not so colorful.

He looked up at a new waitress.

"Hi, my name is Hope. What can I get you to drink, cowboy?"

"Just a water with lemon, and an order to go."

"All right. Need a menu?"

"Nope, I know what I want. Give me a double grass fed burger with bourbon BBQ sauce, lettuce and tomato on a multigrain bun. Rare. Make it rare. Sweet potato fries, too."

"I've got it. Won't be too long. To go, right?"

"Yes, thanks." He wondered if this waitress had a talkative little boy at home who had his sights set on being an actor. That little kid was nothing less than charming.

Brody heard clanking jewelry and the clip-clop of high heels moving closer to his right. That was the only sketchy thing about coming here. Beulah or Annabelle might latch on to you at any minute.

"Well, now, I hope it will take a good long while for your food to come," Annabelle Burton drawled as she hopped up on to the tall chair right beside Brody. She batted her false eyelashes at him and pushed her cleavage together as she crossed her arms and turned toward him.

Brody scooted his chair back a little bit but smiled politely at her. "Hello."

"I was just here for a brunch meeting with the Southern Rose Garden committee. I am so glad I didn't rush right out of here. I would have missed running into you, Brody Bangfield," she said as she set a huge pink leather purse up on the bar.

"Oh, don't let me keep you from your day," Brody said and looked away. He did not like the way she drawled his name out like it had eight syllables.

"No problem at all. I think I can make time for you! I always try to be a good neighbor. I just wanted to say how much I enjoyed watching you with the calves the other day out at the Stetson place. That little boy I brought said on the way home that he wanted to be a Kentucky cowboy just like you! I had just hoped you and I could talk more that day. That's the only thing I would have changed."

Brody silently hoped his meal was almost ready. A rare burger shouldn't take long. He also refrained from asking her about mud being thrown on her or the cars getting stuck in the muddy lower field.

Do not engage.

"Also, you missed the after-church dinner a few weeks ago," she went on. "I was so hoping I could save you a piece of my apple pie. Now, they make a pretty good one here, you know. My momma owns this place and she knows her pie! How about

I run in the back and have them get you a piece to take with you? My treat!"

She laid her hand on his arm and started to hop down from the stool. She leaned up against him as she did.

"Oh! I almost caught my high heel on the bar stool foot rest. You wouldn't have let me fall, would you, Brody?" She finally seemed to right herself and said, "You sure don't say much."

Annabelle was a little too sweet for Brody's tastes and the pie probably was, too.

"No, don't go to any trouble for me. I've got to get back to the farm real soon," he said as he stood up and pulled out some cash while catching Hope's eye.

Annabelle went on while Brody settled the bill, tipped Hope, and picked up his bag of food. She literally talked him right out the door.

"Well, all right, then. I just want you to feel at home here, ok? And, come back soon? Ok?" She was pouring on her unique brand of Kentucky hospitality. He could almost hear her southern drawl getting more pronounced.

"Ok, thanks, ma'am."

"Oh, now, don't call me ma'am - that's so formal. Maybe we could catch a movie or something, sometime, ok? Will you think about that?"

Brody made it out the door just in time to be able to ignore the last questions.

Annabelle Burton had just asked him out. That would have been funny if he had been in a better mood. He looked up as she stuck her head out the door.

"You know where to find me!" She waved goodbye as several different bracelets flashed in the sun.

Next time he would call ahead and order so it would be ready for pick-up.

. . .

As Brody drove back toward Bourbon Creek he wondered how attraction really worked. Did the heart decide who it found interesting and who it didn't? Was it the work of God and the Angels? Was it actually chemistry? He wondered how many books had been written on this subject.

Annabelle might be an attractive girl if you washed off the layers of makeup and took off at least half of her jewelry. But, he couldn't get away from her fast enough. He wondered if she was ever calm and quiet, or wore sensible shoes. He wondered if any man might actually like that flowery perfume. She always wore so much of it.

Yet, from the first moment he laid eyes on Savannah Kay Stetson, he felt like she lived in his heart and his brain. She still did. He felt like she always would. She was interesting and down-to-earth. He wanted to know everything about her.

What a difference!

He headed back to the farm, praying as he drove.

Lord, show me the way. Watch over Savannah for me. Help me to listen and to be patient. I know you've got this. Amen.

Glenwood was laughing at Cinder down near the turn in the long driveway. The dog had a good-sized tree branch in his mouth, dragging it along like it was just a small stick. Brody waved from the open window as he parked the truck nearby.

"Hey, Glenwood."

"Hey."

"I picked up all the supplies we needed."

"Well, thanks, Brody. Oh, before I forget, I want you to come to dinner here at the house on Friday. We'll just order a pizza or something simple. Six-thirty. We will have," Glenwood paused. "A guest."

Cinder gave a quizzical sharp bark and turned his head sideways.

Brody's heart leapt into his throat. "Savannah?"

Glenwood shook his head and said more than Brody had ever heard him say at one time. "No, not that I know of, but she comes and goes all the time, so it wouldn't surprise me. Now, let me get back on track.

"Ok, now, Brody, try to follow this.

"Today a funny thing happened with you, so listen carefully. You. You came up on the porch a little while ago, while you were gone to run errands, and I tried to have a conversation with you, but that wasn't working at all because it wasn't you. But it sure did look like you. It talked like you, too.

"See how you confused me?"

Brody froze. "What? Wait. My brother was here? Here?"

"Yes. Your twin brother, Blaze. Y'all must be identical."

"Only in looks." Brody suddenly pulled on Cinder's tree branch like a tug-of-war with both hands. That dog was so strong.

"Well, anyway, I invited him to eat here on Friday. Son, I want you to feel like you can be comfortable when your relatives come to visit," Glenwood said.

Brody let go of Cinder's tree branch and the silence seemed awkward.

"Brody?"

"Well, I won't be comfortable at all. He hasn't called or texted me." Brody fidgeted with the feed store supply list, picking at the edges of the horse stickers. *He hasn't apologized ever in his life, either, for anything.* "He's supposed to be in Montana. What was he doing here? Did he say?"

"He didn't say. I didn't hardly give him time to try. I thought it was YOU and just jumped right in to talking about that ornery old bull, Bruno, and what were we going to do with him? Your brother actually had some interesting ideas about that and talked to me like he WAS you for a good while. But, his smile wasn't exactly like yours and I finally realized..."

"I'm sorry he messed with you like that. It's sure not the first time."

Brody suddenly had a bad feeling in his gut. He was wondering how long his brother had been in this area of the country.

"We on for Friday?" Glenwood persisted.

Brody sighed. It seemed like Glenwood really wanted him to have pizza with him and his twin brother. "Ok, I'll be here, but I can't promise I'll stay very long," he said.

"Fair enough," the older man chuckled.

"Hey, Glenwood, if you give him any bourbon, give him the cheap stuff."

Glenwood threw his head back in a belly laugh. "You bet!"

Brody took a deep breath and said, "That'll make it better somehow. Ok, I'd better get busy. I'm gonna unload the feed store stuff into the barn and the feed shed."

"Thanks, Brody."

Did Blaze actually ask Dad where I was? Why would he bother? What would bring him here? Bull riding business, maybe?

CHAPTER 22

Savannah turned the stuffed chair toward the window and dropped down into it. She pulled her feet up to the side and looked out the window. Her second floor view showed the building across from hers, exactly mirroring this one. She could see the sidewalk and parking lot through the rain along with three garbage cans and only one scraggly tree.

She had absolutely nothing to do and she wasn't used to that.

The sound of yet another siren annoyed her. She could hear lots of traffic noise from here, and the muffled voices and TVs from her neighbors. Other than that, the night was quiet behind the rain hitting the windows.

Thin windows. Thin walls.

I guess I could go to that little bar that's just a couple of blocks away. I want to like it there but I don't want to run into that rude guy. He seemed to always be hanging out. He wouldn't leave me alone yesterday. He thought he was quite a show pony, buying me a drink and getting mad when I wouldn't talk to him. I didn't like how he laughed when I told him to hold his horses and back it up. He was giving me the creeps.

I don't feel like talking to anyone.

So, I guess I don't need to go out in the rain to sit at a bar.

I don't want the smell of cigarette smoke in my hair anyway.

I guess that settles it.

She looked down at the sound of her phone. Lana wanted to FaceTime, again.

She let it ring until it stopped. Then she texted, "About to get in the shower. Talk later." She couldn't even talk to her best friend right now. She couldn't bear how hard Lana tried to cheer her up.

She missed her dearest friend.

Lana, I need a little more silence. I know you will understand.

She sipped her ginger tea and decided to stay in tonight. Tea would be enough and she wouldn't have to face the rain just for a little bourbon.

It had rained all day long while she looked for a job earlier. It had rained in her heart for almost two weeks since she had left Cinder and daddy and, of course, Brody.

It seemed like getting a decent job here wasn't going to be as easy as she had thought. She would start fresh in the morning.

She could always substitute teach in the public schools when they started back after their summer break, but the money was not good at all. No banks seemed to be hiring around here. She wasn't in a good enough mood to even think about being a waitress. Maybe a customer service job would be bearable, at least for a while.

I guess I'm meant to be alone forever, just like my daddy.

Brody was just several weeks of distraction and excitement and happiness. I should have known better.

I don't know what to do. I wonder if daddy ever felt this alone when mom left. Maybe he did and just hid it from me. Maybe he keeps a happy face on all the time and still longs for mom, and talks to her in his head?

Oh, I hope not.

I can't imagine feeling this downhearted for that long.

I wonder if mom ever looks back and regrets leaving? I guess I'll never know. I should text her soon and ask how she's doing and if she might come visit soon. I'd love for her to meet Brody -

What am I doing?

What am I doing here?

I thought leaving would be exciting and adventurous. I thought I would meet possible new boyfriends everywhere I looked. What is wrong with my decision-making?

I hate this.

Every time I turn around I just hit another wall. I can't seem to get anywhere with my life. I don't know what to do. How am I supposed to know where to turn? There's nothing for me here. Nothing.

I hate to be wrong.

Tears trickled down her face as she watched it rain. She started sniffling and knew a big pity-party ugly cry was just seconds away. Well, why not? What else did she have to do?

She gave up on the plan to take a long hot bubble bath or even a shower. She just didn't have the energy to bother. Who cared, anyway?

She slowly got up and closed the blinds on the window. She pulled back the quilt on the bed and leaned back against the headboard. She shoved her stack of books and planners over and hugged her favorite pillow that she had brought with her.

Then, she cried.

She cried for the beloved land she had left. She cried for her dad and her friends. She cried for her chestnut beauty, Buttercup, and dear sweet Cinder. She even missed the Young Farmers group and her boring job at the bank.

She cried for being alone at the ripe old age of twenty-six with no goals or plans for her successful future.

She cried even harder when she allowed herself to face the fact that she wanted to go home, even if it meant the heartache of running into Brody.

Maybe I should have fought for him.

Maybe I should have rushed down those stairs at the concert and pulled that redhead's hand out of his and kissed him in front of her and dared him not to respond to me.

I guess I just gave him to the mysterious redhead when I stormed away that Sunday morning. Maybe I should have confronted him at the Young Farmers Day with what I saw and given him one more chance. Maybe we could have talked it out?

No, it was over before it really began...

When will I ever stop going over it in my mind?

Her crying began to subside little by little. Maybe the stress release would help her sleep. She hoped so.

She got up to rinse out the big mug she'd been drinking tea out of. She even found the discipline to wash her face and brush her teeth.

She was going to look rough tomorrow with her swollen eyes.

Oh, well.

Maybe tomorrow she would find a job, make some friends, and enjoy living here for a little while longer. Maybe.

She texted Lana that she was completely exhausted and heading for bed and could they just talk in a day or two. Then she crawled into bed and turned her phone on silent.

CHAPTER 23

Friday night rolled around quickly and Brody found himself having dinner with Glenwood and his brother. He had dreaded this, but he had to admit that it wasn't nearly as bad as he had thought it would be.

It was still confusing though.

Glenwood looked from Brody to Blaze and then back again. "Your mom and dad must have had a tough time raising the two of you. It's uncanny how much you two look and sound alike. Oh, it must have been hard on your friends to keep you straight!"

Blaze smiled his sly fox smile. "Friends, and girlfriends, too." He shot Brody a look that held a lot of history.

Brody did not take the bait. He thought the conversation had been shallow all evening and still didn't know what his brother was doing here in Kentucky, except to brag on himself. He guessed it was time to ask.

"Blaze, what are you doing here in Kentucky? It's not like you to just come for a visit. Too busy for that, aren't you?"

Blaze ignored his brother and turned to Glenwood. "We're

actually different in lots of ways. I was always braver. Once I found I could stay on two thousand pounds of muscle-bound bull, I knew I'd found a way to fuel my need for thrills and pad my bank account, too."

Glenwood stopped his slice of pizza in mid-air. "Is that why you're here in

central Kentucky? The Professional Bull Riders Tour will be in Rupp Arena sometime next month, right?"

"Well, Mr Stetson, I don't mean to brag-"

"Yes, you do," Brody interrupted.

Blaze went on. "See, I've won about all the tours I'd need to for a lifetime. I'm just checking out some bulls for an international client this trip. Everyone doesn't understand the concerns of social dominance in bulls on a farm and this client knew I would be a business asset to his purchasing power.

"But, you're right, Mr Stetson. I'll be back for that very tour. They've hired me on this year as an announcer. Now, I'm not doing all 34 cities, just, let's see, five shows in Las Vegas, two in Utah, one in South Dakota, and a couple in Billings, Montana. We're still negotiating for New Mexico and Arizona."

Brody tried not to roll his eyes and said, "So, Kentucky's not really your usual hunting grounds, that's for sure."

He watched Glenwood reach across the table for yet another piece of pizza. He couldn't resist putting another slice of sausage, red onion, and extra cheese pizza on his paper plate, too.

"Blaze? Finish it up?"

"Oh, no. I'd better stop while I can still get up from the table." Blaze patted his six-pack abs and smiled.

"Discipline," said Glenwood.

"Only with food," Brody couldn't help saying.

"I would have to agree that Brody is the more disciplined, more practical twin," Blaze said to Glenwood. "If I were more disciplined, I wouldn't have this aching hip from the bull-riding days. I do like excess when it comes to many things, like exotic cowboy boots, and travel, and redheads."

"Oh, Glenwood, Blaze even has specialty cowboy boots named after him - there really is a Blaze Bangfield boot," Brody said, a bit sarcastically.

"Well, it's great to share a pizza with such a famous bull-rider. Nowadays, I feel really lucky to have Brody here as our Master Herdsman and property manager. He has fit into the routines easily and big things are getting done at a very impressive rate," Glenwood bragged to Blaze. "Lord willing and the creek don't rise, Brody will be around here a long time helping to increase our calf crop. Bluegrass fed beef!"

Blaze stared at his brother. "Hmm. This is where I say I'm happy for you. And you say you are happy for me, right?"

Brody said, "Sure thing. Now, let's have a little bourbon and call it a night."

Brody had been on his best behavior, but it was hard not to fall into old habits when his brother came around bragging about himself up one side and down the other. Sometimes he felt like he was twelve years old again, resenting his brother's every move.

Glenwood looked again at the identical twins at his table. "Brody, why don't you pour us all a shot? You can choose from either of the two bottles that are out." He winked at Brody.

Brody hadn't heard of either of these before when he went to the bar. They were the only two bottles out. Good old Glenwood! These must be two cheaper bourbons, just like he had asked. He would have to thank him later.

He sat back down as he handed his older brother the drink, and asked, "How's dad?"

Blaze threw back the bourbon in one gulp and sat the glass on the table. "Pretty good last I saw him."

Brody tasted his bourbon. It was as good as most any other, to him. "When was that?"

"Oh, a couple of weeks ago. I've been in Lexington for almost two weeks."

"Did it take two weeks to help an international client buy some bulls?"

"You see, he got caught up with business in Italy, so I took some time to observe his bulls properly, to gage what he should buy for the best genetic improvement. Now, I also found a redhead to keep me company until he got back here." There was that sly fox smile again.

Brody's heart nearly knocked its way out of his chest. "A redhead? Huh." He narrowed his eyes at Blaze. "Did you catch any of the Kentucky local music scene while you wined and dined her?"

"I sure did. This little lady talked me into seeing several local acts in bars around the whole area. We also saw... what was it? Backtrack? Backwoods?"

Brody stood up. "Backroad? The Country Music Backroad Show?"

Blaze stared at his brother. "Yeah. That's it. Great show. Did you see it?"

Brody nearly choked. "No, I didn't."

"You should have. Best thing there was Emily Jamison and the color of her hair. Not exactly red, but more of a strawberry blond."

Brody suddenly pulled his brother up from the table and threw his arms around him in a big bear hug. He patted his shoulders happily before letting go.

"What in the world has gotten into you, Brody?" Blaze questioned his brother. "You are never, um, affectionate with me."

"Well, it's been great to talk to you tonight, Blaze, my dear brother! Wow. You and Glenwood have fun tomorrow with

troublesome old Bruno. I won't be able to be here. Is that ok?"
Brody turned toward Glenwood.

"Well, I guess we could put it off -"

Blaze cut him off. "No need for that. I'll be glad to help Mr Stetson with Bruno in the morning. I have to be in this area a couple more days. I'd be much better at it than you, anyway, Brody."

Brody laughed and looked at Glenwood. "See what I mean?"

Glenwood held up his hands to them both, staying out of it.

Brody turned back to his slightly older brother. "Ok, um, thanks, Blaze. Seriously, thanks a lot."

Blaze sat back down, surprised at Brody's affection. "No problem. I probably owe you a favor, or two."

Brody laughed. "More like twelve, but I'll take it!"

Glenwood asked, "Brody, why can't you help us?"

Brody was already halfway across the room and heading for the door. He looked back and smiled. "Something's come up. Something really important and time-sensitive!"

He headed out onto the porch, then turned back around. "Hey, Glenwood. Ok if I get a puppy?"

Glenwood laughed. "Heck, fire, get two if you want."

As the door slammed, Blaze said, "What was that all about?"

"Not quite sure."

"Well, I had better head back to my hotel. Thanks for the hospitality," Blaze said.

"All right. I'll see you bright and early, then. It'll be interesting to see what a famous bull rider like you will think of that cranky bull of mine. Thanks, Blaze. Thanks a lot. You've been a really big help tonight."

"No problem. I'll see myself out." Blaze picked up his Stetson hat as he headed for the door.

"Good night."

Glenwood felt like he had watched the brothers get a little closer to each other and that was a good thing.

He also had a feeling that there had been a bad case of mistaken identity somewhere along the line, but he was pretty confident now that Brody and Savannah would find their way back to each other soon. That would make all of them happier.

He was going to sleep well tonight.

CHAPTER 24

The early morning held great promise as Brody turned Paulo toward the barn. He had already had a good ride before the sun came up. It was a time for clearing his head, working on problems, and thanking God for his many blessings.

Today he had a plan to raise the standards in his life and check off many things on his new to-do list.

This day was a new day and the old hymn There Shall Be Showers of Blessings was stuck in his head.

He texted Savannah a short message. It said "I have figured it all out. We must talk soon, face to face."

He hoped she would read it but he wasn't sure she would. She hadn't answered any of his other texts or picked up the phone when he called yet.

So, he needed to go see her, but he still didn't know where she was.

Next on his mental list was to go see Malachi Ford, Lana's brother. He wanted to take a look at those puppies as soon as possible. Somehow it seemed really important to take care of that right now.

Even though it was still early morning, he picked up his phone and called the number he had taken from the feed supply store bulletin board.

Malachi Ford answered and told him to come on over right now to see if he might like one of the puppies.

Brody headed toward the address. It was only about fifteen minutes away.

He turned off the curving blacktop road onto a dirt road with some gravel here and there. There was a large pond and fields of soybeans as far as the eye could see.

The house was small and solid, with white painted brick and a black roof and shutters. It sat back from the main road just enough to be a nice, quiet place. Red petunias grew in front of the porch. Brody liked it instantly.

A small metal building sat just behind the house. It had a double garage door that was going up as Brody drove closer and a man stepped out and waved. He was wearing overalls over a big and solid body. He didn't look a thing like Lana.

The two men hit it off immediately. They were comfortable talking about cattle, Ford trucks, and dogs. Malachi led Brody around back to a large and very tall fenced-in yard.

Four black and tan puppies yipped at the gate, jumping and trying to get all of Malachi's attention. The high energy was infectious.

The men got the gate closed behind them and Brody sat down in the middle of the wiggling mass of puppies. They were climbing all over him as he said, "Oh, you all smell Cinder on me, don't you?"

Delta, their mom, lay down on the other side of Malachi, glad for a short break. Malachi squatted down and scratched her behind her ears as he said, "One night I heard the neighbor's coonhounds running loose. They were baying up along the ridge back there." He pointed to the south ridgeline. "I figured they were chasing deer. There's a redbone and a black and tan; good dogs. Anyway, I went back to sleep. I didn't know it then, but Delta here climbed this fence and took off after them."

"This fence? Wow." Brody was impressed.

"Oh, yeah," Malachi went on. "I came out here the next morning to let her come into the house but she wasn't in the fence. She was laying in the front porch swing and seemed very pleased with herself."

Brody laughed. "And look what happened."

"Yeah, since she was in heat, I lost out on a litter of full-blooded german shepherd puppy money. I was planning on having one litter, maybe two, and then get her fixed. I guess she had plans of her own though."

"Well, she sure is pretty."

"Yep. She's a good girl. Her pups seem to be fine animals; clever, playful, and smart. There's two girls and two boys. I can't keep them all. Lana vouched for you, so that's good enough for me."

"That's nice. She told me you might not say more than ten words, total," Brody said.

"I've used up a month's worth of talking on you. Anyway, you like any of them?"

Brody liked the same one he had noticed most in the photo. Black and tan with one ear up and one ear flopping over, tail wagging, and it was a girl. Yep, this was the one.

"I like this one here the most. I think she might like me, too." Brody felt of her fluffy body.

"Heck, they all seem to like you! What do you want a puppy for? Glenwood not keeping you busy enough?" Malachi laughed.

Brody went with the truth. "Well, I think I need the love of a good dog in my life. I think Cinder will help me train her. And, I think Savannah will come home, love the puppy, and then we will live happily ever after. Sound good?"

Malachi nodded his head. "That would make my sister happy, too. It would be great if you could make that happen."

"I'll do my best. That's all I can do."

"Back in high school, I'd go to the Stetson's farm and work with the Young Farmers program. Glenwood taught me a lot."

"He is still knee-deep in all of that. Well, what do I owe you? You should let me pay you something for my new dog."

"Naw. Your money's no good here."

"Well, thank you. I'll take good care of her. Are you calling her anything yet?"

"Been calling her Chance. You name her whatever you take a liking to. She can keep the collar, but it won't fit her for long. Sure you don't want two dogs? They could keep each other company."

Brody shook his head. "I think one will be enough. If you want to come out and see her sometime, I'd like that. Bring Delta, too."

Malachi nodded. "I might take you up on that."

Brody had only just met Lana's brother, but he felt like he would be a real friend in no time at all. So, he went with his gut and asked him a question. "Hey, Malachi, I want to go see Savannah. I've got to talk to her. We've had a big misunderstanding. Big. You know what that's like with a woman?"

Malachi picked up Chance and gave her a big affectionate hug. "I surely do and it's no fun at all."

"Do you know where Savannah is, Malachi? Because I don't."

"Naw, but Lana knows. Just call her up."

"I need her number." He picked up his new puppy and headed toward his truck where the leash was waiting.

"I'll give it to you. You tell her I said to help you out." Malachi grinned as he pulled out his phone from his overalls pocket. "I have to look up my only sister's number. Once it goes in the phone, it goes out of my head."

CHAPTER 25

*S*avannah tied up her shoes and stretched her calves. She seemed to never have time for a run, but living here gave her plenty of time. So, she would put it to good use. You couldn't job-hunt twenty-four hours a day.

She planned to run 2 whole miles in one direction and then turn around. Next, she would walk until she caught her breath and then run the rest of the way back. Four miles would be her target.

She swung her left leg back and forth and then her right leg. She knew she had better loosen her hips and get the blood flowing. This Saturday morning run would be just what she needed to clear her head, work on her plans, and not look at Brody's last text even one more time.

She had it memorized anyway.

"I have figured it all out. We must talk soon, face to face."

She had read it a hundred times! What could he possibly mean by that?

Figured what out? How to try to lie your way out of what I saw with my very own eyes? I don't think so!

She took off down the sidewalk at much too fast a pace, hoping that punishing her body with a grueling run would stop the endless circle her mind kept running around and around in.

She looked both ways at every street, but it wasn't busy this early around here. Her ponytail bounced with her fast pacing as she tried to focus on her steps. *Breathe in for four strides, hold my breath for four strides, and breath out for six, no, seven strides. Well, girl, that won't last long. Adjust your numbers down. You need oxygen.*

She could not seem to find the rhythm in her running. She looked around for distractions but there wasn't much to look at.

Ok, run hard to the next mailbox then do a recovery jog to the next one. Ugh! I hate to run. I feel like I've been running forever.

"I have it all figured out. We must talk soon, face to face."

STOP it!

She was panting like she was finishing a half-marathon at not quite the half-mile mark, so she slowed to a walk just as her phone rang.

She looked down at her phone and tried to catch her breath. It was Lana. She had put her off too much lately so she answered the call.

She didn't want to run anyway.

"Hey, girl." Savannah slowed her walk down even more and turned back toward her little rental.

"You sound like someone is chasing you. What are you doing?" There was concern in Lana's voice.

"I'm going for a four-mile run, while I have the time."

"Why on earth would you want to do that?"

"I don't know. I haven't found a job yet and the place I'm staying in is very clean and neat as a pin," Savannah said. "I'm glad you called though. I really didn't want to run four miles."

"You sound bored enough to come home! Right? Am I right?"

Lana. Always the encourager.

"I don't know. Sometimes I feel like I'm leaning that way. Life is short, right? That's what everyone says. So, maybe it is time to come home, at least for a good visit. I miss you all so much." Savannah felt the truth in the words she had just said.

Lana was practically jumping up and down in her laundry room. She nearly knocked over the huge stack of sheets and towels she had just folded. She righted them as she said, "You would make your daddy so happy. I'm not really being selfish here. How about you come for a visit tomorrow and see how it feels? We could catch a movie or shop or eat gluten-free pizza. Then we could go pet all the puppies in the Main Street pet shop. What do you say? Or, we could run to Malachi's and play with his puppies. Oh! If you get up super early you could surprise your daddy at church."

Savannah loved hearing the enthusiasm in her friend's voice. "Ok. Slow down. I will come for a visit tomorrow. I'll text you when I head out, ok? I don't know how early I'll get on the road."

"Perfect. Oh, something else I should mention," Lana said. "Brody came by the bank the other day."

Savannah frowned. "Well, he banks there, so that's no big deal."

Lana laughed. "He made sure he got in my line."

Savannah slowed down her walking even more. "Why are we talking about Brody?"

"Well, he asked me to tell him why you won't talk to him and help him get you to come home. I think he is still crazy about you. Like, for real."

"You didn't tell him where I am, did you?" Savannah stopped walking.

"No. I didn't tell him anything... really."

"Ok, thanks. Well, I'd better go. I'm just so crazy busy here, you know."

Lana laughed. "If you say so. See you tomorrow! Come to my place first!"

"You bet. Bye."

As Savannah got close to her little rental she checked the red heart on her phone. She had put in just over eight-tenths of one mile. It sure wasn't four miles, but, for now, it was good enough.

CHAPTER 26

Glenwood sat astride Paulo and expertly cut a few cows from the herd. He used as little movement as possible, confident in his abilities. Decades of practice gave a man success in things like that.

The small group headed toward the gate from Blaze's gentle pressure, cutting back and forth from behind. The cows were cooperating well this morning, following the natural flow of the first cow to get moving.

Blaze had shown up that morning with a plan to move Bruno out of the pasture he was in. Glenwood would be on his horse, and Blaze in the John Deere gator, but Glenwood put that plan out of their possible choices, explaining how keyed up Bruno always got from any machinery like vehicles and tractors.

"The younger bulls would be fine that way, Blaze, but not Bruno. Gators, and four-wheelers can't go sideways, either, and that always makes me nervous when trying to deal with any bull. You just never know what kind of mood they will be in."

"Ok, you know Bruno better than I do. I've always liked going into a pasture with a Gator. If a bull gets riled up for some reason, you can use it for cover, or even jump in it from either side and drive away."

"That's very true, but a good horse will pretty much do the same thing."

Blaze was riding Buttercup.

"You think he's hurt in some way we can't see?" Blaze asked.

Glenwood shook his head. "I had him checked out thoroughly before I bought him and once since I've had him here, too. I was concerned about the same thing, but they didn't find a thing."

"I guess he's just as cranky as they come."

Glenwood agreed. "He is that. I'm glad you got a chance to see him jumping around like he's gone half-crazy this morning, up close and personal. I used to read the story of Ferdinand the Bull to Savannah when she was little, and that's what he reminds me of!"

"It would have been hard to adequately describe Bruno's bucking around, for sure!" Blaze said. "Hey, I think we are working pretty well here together. Brody didn't need to worry about our teamwork." Blaze leaned toward a gate.

Buttercup was an extraordinary gate-horse. She knew the clanking sounds from opening and shutting gates was nothing to worry about. Blaze wondered if he could buy her. He would love to own her, or maybe one of her foals in the future, at the very least.

Glenwood looked over at Blaze. "Well, it's almost like I am working with Brody. I got used to your brother pretty quick. He knows how to read animals. He's even good on the ground with the herds, walking to their flight zone so calmly. They always move away from his pressure just like he wants them to."

"He was born with a gift for working a balance point," Blaze said.

Glenwood chuckled. He would have to remember to tell

Brody that his brother actually bragged on him today, and it wasn't sarcastic at all.

"And you were born crazy enough to try to stay on a raging bull for eight seconds!" Glenwood added.

"I sure was. It used to worry my mom to death." Blaze went back toward the cows to bring another group up to the gate.

The men had decided if Bruno didn't want to move pastures today, they would just try to move the cows instead, out of there and away from him.

So far, Bruno was ok with the idea.

As they headed back, they talked about managing bulls.

"I usually keep 3 bulls in a big pasture. I find it increases conception rates," Glenwood said. "Competition works."

"Bet you always have to keep Bruno as a lone bull in the pasture. He seems like a fighter, and fighting and defending territory doesn't exactly keep his mind on servicing his lady cows," Blaze laughed. "Maybe he should be in the bull-riding circuit."

"He might be too old. I don't know about those details."

"We could talk about that over lunch? I am starving! Can I buy you lunch somewhere in town?"

"You wouldn't have to twist my arm, but it seems like I'd better pick up the check, since you're helping me out today while your brother goes out looking for love in all the right places."

Blaze looked over at Glenwood with the sly fox smile. "Care to elaborate?"

"Maybe at lunch," Glenwood laughed.

CHAPTER 27

*B*rody hooked the leash on Chance's collar just before the puppy leaped out of his truck. He walked her in the grass beside the grocery store parking lot. She wagged her tail and seemed to sniff every weed within reach.

Brody mentally clicked off tasks he had taken care of so far this morning. His truck was clean. He had on a shirt and jeans that Savannah had complimented him on a couple of weeks ago. He had a puppy for her to meet.

I'll be surprised if Chance doesn't pull on Savannah's heartstrings. She sure does mine. Smart little fur-ball with her funny ears and big feet. She is a sweet pup.

He had been in the grocery store earlier. He had asked the girl at the floral counter to put two big bouquets of flowers together and add a huge bow. He also had her make a big matching bow to hook onto Chance's collar for when they got there.

Surely that would catch Savannah's attention, and maybe make an impression of just how important she was to him. She was all about the details.

He had finally found the courage to call Lana and talk

Savannah's address out of her. It hadn't been nearly as hard as he thought it would be. Life was like that sometimes - the dread was much worse than just facing things and getting them taken care of.

Lana had asked him what his plan was. He had told her he was going to just show up, with a huge bouquet of flowers and a puppy. He would get her attention somehow. He would wait beside her car or wait by her door until she came out. He would sing cowboy songs up to her windows - whatever he needed to do. He planned to tell Savannah he had an identical twin brother who had been at the Country Music Backroad Show with a redhead. Mistaken identity might sound cliche, but it was reality in his life!

Lana wished him luck and sounded like she really meant it.

Oh, Savannah. I should have found a way to convince you that I was at home, before you took off!

He had the address plugged into the maps app on his phone.

He had beef jerky and water in the car.

He and Chance made their way back to the truck so Brody could give the puppy a drink of water, too. She sloshed and slurped the water and then put both front paws into the bowl and pawed at it, sloshing out the last of the water.

Brody laughed at her antics and helped her up into the truck. "Lay down, Chance. Good girl!"

He popped a mint into his mouth and started up the truck.

It was time to get on the road.

All roads lead to Savannah Kay Stetson.

CHAPTER 28

*G*lenwood and Blaze slid into a mahogany leather booth at the Cowtown Diner. Glenwood picked up the menu and watched Blaze look all around.

"I can appreciate the cool feel of this place. It's beautiful. Nice choice, Mr Stetson."

"Decor hasn't got anything to do with it. The best grass-fed burgers anywhere? That's what I'm talking about, right here in our little town," Glenwood said.

"Well, that's high praise, now. I've eaten some fine grass fed burgers in my day," said Blaze. "So, you said you were going to elaborate about my brother looking for love in all the right places?"

"Maybe." Glenwood didn't think for a minute that Blaze would forget this topic of conversation.

"Anyone you know?" Blaze leaned in closer.

Glenwood laughed. "Yes, for sure, and it might even be my kinfolk."

"Interesting," Blaze said.

A waitress headed toward them just as Miss Annabelle

Burton waved the girl away and headed there herself. Her hips swayed along with tiny steps from such high heels.

"Well, look what the cat dragged in. It must be my lucky day! Brody Bangfield, in the flesh, and Mr Stetson? Too bad my mom is not here to flirt with you, Mr. Stetson." She laughed a little too loudly. Her bracelets jingled as she gestured and then put her hands on her hips in a practiced pose.

Blaze and Glenwood exchanged a look that said a lot more than Annabelle might notice.

Blaze decided then and there to have a little innocent fun and let her continue to think he was Brody. He looked Annabelle over slowly, from her silver sandals up to her big eyes. "Are you here to flirt with me?" he asked as his eyes twinkled with unspoken fun.

Annabelle put both hands on the table and looked just a little bit rattled, as if she wasn't expecting that response at all.

"Well, I might be, although it hasn't done me much good yet." She shot a quizzical look at Glenwood.

Blaze wiggled his eyebrows at Glenwood and then stood up. He took Annabelle in his arms and quickly pulled her in close. He kissed her thoroughly but quickly, bending her backwards. Then, just as quickly, he sat back down.

Dizzy from an unexpected kiss like that, Annabelle slowly opened her eyes. She just stared at Blaze as if she were too shocked to even remember to breathe.

Blaze noticed this and asked Glenwood what her name was.

"Miss Annabelle Burton," Glenwood laughed.

Blaze looked up an Annabelle. "Miss Annabelle Burton," he said in his deepest voice. "You best start breathing again, or you might pass out." He nodded his head, encouraging her.

Annabelle shook her head and when she finally took a breath she made a little gasping sound. "Ooh!" she squeaked.

Glenwood shook his head at the antics taking place right in front of him.

Blaze wouldn't admit it out loud, but he was surprised by how much he had enjoyed having this woman in his arms. Surprising, since she was not exactly his type.

"Well, I declare." She put her fingertips to her lips.

Glenwood thought it was time to tell her who this was. "Annabelle, this is not Brody Bangfield -"

"Now, Glenwood, that is silly," she interrupted, not taking her eyes off of Blaze.

"I'd like for you to meet his identical twin brother, Blaze Bangfield," Glenwood finished.

The men waited for Annabelle to respond.

"God made two of you?" She bit her lip, looking deeply into Blaze's blue eyes.

"Yes, he did." Blaze politely put out his hand to shake hers and went on. "I'm very pleased to meet you, Annabelle. Now, would you care to join us for lunch?" He hadn't let go of her hand.

"No. I couldn't possibly... yes, I'd like.... no, really, I can't right now. Oh, my goodness!"

"Could I please have a raincheck?" He asked as he finally let go of her hand.

"Um-hmm," she said as she shuffled toward the kitchen, looking back over her shoulder again and again.

The waitress came back over and took care of everything.

They enjoyed the food while the conversation turned once again to the brothers. Glenwood felt that talking through their grievances might help both Blaze and Brody, so he did his best to get Blaze to open up to him.

"Tell me something about Brody that I might need to know," Glenwood encouraged.

Blaze seemed happy to oblige. "Ok. Good or bad?"

"Both if you want."

"Brody is patient with all animals and most people. He is

never patient with me. Never. I've known how to push his buttons his whole life. It's a wonder he ever talks to me.

"He got the wrong idea about dad leaving the ranch all to just me. I let him. Heck, I helped him come to that conclusion, but that's not what dad said at all. He said I should have the whole ranch, and I should buy Brody out of his half.

"Brody has walked away from it all. I let him do that, but it's starting to gnaw on me. He doesn't like confrontation, so he walks.

"Part of why I'm here is to explain all this to him. I want to know if he will be ok with this plan for me to buy him out.

"Dad has had the ranch's market value estimated by professional appraisers so I can have a dollar amount to work toward. I have a sizable check for him this trip. I just haven't given it to him yet."

"Why?" asked Glenwood.

"No fun in that. Old habits die hard," Blaze laughed.

CHAPTER 29

*S*avannah sat with her laptop, sipping afternoon coffee and searching for work-from-home online jobs. She didn't like the sound of any of these. Nothing looked promising at all. Besides, the wifi in there was as slow as mud.

She wondered how in the world a day could drag on as long as this one. It was as if the clock had just slowed to a crawl.

She was hungry. Again.

Would Sunday morning never come?

She had driven over to a little coffee shop that had a decent view of the town square. Two little kids were chasing down a ball in the grass while their mom looked at her phone. None of the people on the sidewalks seemed to be in a hurry. Small town Saturday was alive and well.

She'd found this coffee shop as soon as she had left the farm. It had big stuffed chairs and an eclectic mix of painted tables and mismatched straight-back chairs that seemed to have been painted by several different folklore painters. The frames on the walls held black and white photography - coffee themed close-ups and kitchen essentials.

It was a good place to be near people, but not have to talk to them. The music they played here was an ever-changing mix of new pop and folk music along with bluegrass. She had brought her headphones the first visit, but found she didn't need them here.

She felt as comfortable in this local coffee shop as she was going to get.

I just want to go see Lana. I want to hug daddy and hang out at the house for a while and have Cinder leaning against me while I scratch behind his ears.

Home.

Maybe if I take a ride on Buttercup I'll get to see Brody from afar. Maybe he'll be checking fence-line, with his back muscles straining his shirt seams. His rugged face will be set in concentration. Maybe he will look up at me and smile and start walking toward me. He will just drop everything when he sees me. He will get really close to me... and I will... YELL AT HIM FOR BEING WITH THAT STUPID GORGEOUS REDHEAD.

Come on, girl!

SHE WAS BORED with online job-hunting. Next, she tried to find some interesting documentary to watch but nothing really caught her attention.

Maybe she should just head back home now. Today. Why wait until tomorrow? She could leave from here since most of her clothes were at home anyway.

Let's see. I have on my favorite tennis shoes and I have my planner. There's a mascara in my purse. I have a toothbrush there and another good pillow.

That settles it.

I'll go home now. I'll hang out with dad tonight and go to church in the morning and then do all the things with Lana after that. It will be fun to surprise her by getting there sooner than she is expecting.

I'll stay WAY too busy to think much about Brody Whatever-Your-Middle-Name-Is Bangfield!

She pocketed her phone and gathered up her laptop. Then, with her new plan in mind, she grabbed a coffee for the road from the barista. After tipping him, she headed toward her car.

She knew she had just made the right decision.

She was surprised how much better she already felt.

CHAPTER 30

*G*lenwood had to convince Blaze that this meal was his treat, but they didn't argue about it for long. Blaze finally gave in.

Then Blaze surprised him yet again.

"Hey, you care if I come on behind you about 20 minutes? There's something I'd like to take care of while I'm in town."

Glenwood nodded. "That's fine, but if you want me to wait, I don't care to, at all."

Blaze shook his head. "No, it's ok. Really."

"But your truck is at my farm. You remember that, right?"

"I know. No worries." Blaze wasn't moving from the booth, even after Glenwood paid the check and stood up to leave.

"Alrighty then. See you in a little bit," Glenwood said.

He wondered what this was about but decided it wasn't really any of his business. It could be personal, and besides, it seemed like Blaze was capable of getting back out to the farm on his own. Maybe Blaze was going to mess with poor Annabelle some more. Maybe he was going to flirt with the waitress now. Neither one of those would surprise him.

"I won't be long," Blaze smiled up at him. "Don't worry about me."

"Ok. It's Saturday anyway. There's no time clock."

Glenwood headed out of the cool dark interior of the diner and into the afternoon sunshine. He reached for his sunglasses and headed for his truck.

He turned back out onto the road while he thought about what else he could work on today. He probably had time to go through the mail and email. He would text Savannah again. Darn daughter was always flying off the handle and taking off to parts unknown. She was smart though. She would probably make her way home soon enough.

Maybe he would wait for Blaze to check on how Bruno was doing. Glenwood's belly was full and he counted his many blessings as he drove along. It didn't do anyone any good to worry about things. Better to lay it at the feet of Jesus and keep moving forward.

He yawned and thought maybe he could even catch a catnap in the hammock until at least one of those identical twins showed up.

CHAPTER 31

*B*rody pulled into the parking lot and shut off the truck while looking all around. Savannah's temporary address looked safe enough. It was clean and in a decent part of town. Brody was relieved about that.

So, this is where she's been hiding out.

Where are you, Savannah? Please, you've got to listen to me today.

Little Chance woke up and yawned and stretched in the seat beside him. The windows were down about three inches. She stuck her nose as far out as she could and whined.

Brody turned off his phone's maps app and said, "I hear you, Miss Chance. Let's take a little walk around the block. I don't see Savannah's car here anyway. Come on. Good puppy."

After Brody went around the entire neighborhood, he wound up carrying the puppy back part of the way.

"Oh, you're going to have to work on your endurance, little girl. Cinder will want to run you all over the farm soon."

He sat in the grass with his back against a small tree and took off his hat. The puppy was panting in the shade and laid across his boots so that he could rub her belly.

He saw a curtain move at one of the windows.

A few minutes later, a middle-aged lady came out of a door along the front of the place. She headed right toward him.

"Oh, can I pet your dog?" she asked, while already petting Chance.

"Sure. She doesn't seem to mind," Brody said.

"I'm Hazel. I live in number four." She smiled. "I'm heading out to work. Can I help you with anything?"

"No, ma'am. I'm just waiting for Savannah Stetson, in number three," Brody answered.

"Oh! I've talked to her a little. She's not here," Hazel stated the obvious. "Probably at the coffee shop on 17th street."

"Well, I might just drive over there. I don't want my flowers to wilt... or my dog," Brody said.

Hazel laughed. "It's supposed to be a hot one today. Anyway, the place is called Roasted. You can't miss it. Well, I'd better get to work."

Brody settled his hat back on his head and stood up. "Thanks so much. You have a nice day, Hazel."

The lady just stood there, as if she really didn't want to leave at all. "I'll be sure and tell Savannah I saw you, in case you don't find her," Hazel finally said.

"I appreciate that, but I really do need to find her. Today."

CHAPTER 32

*B*laze sat alone in the booth and waved the waitress over again.

"Y'all forget anything?" she asked.

"Not exactly. I was wondering if you could help me with something." Blaze gave his best smile.

"Maybe..." Hope hedged.

Blaze laughed. "I was wondering if you could tell me if that little Annabelle Burton was still back in the kitchen."

"Last I looked, she was peeking through the swinging door and watching your every move." Hope nodded her head slightly over one shoulder.

"Oh, I think I see what you mean," Blaze said. "Could you ask her to bring me her favorite dessert? And, I would love if she would join me?"

"I'll go check on that." Hope hurried back to the kitchen smiling all the way.

After a few minutes Annabelle came out carrying an entire apple pie on the flat of her right hand. She had a knife and two plates in the left. Her cheeks were flushed a bright pink.

"Apple pie," he said. "That's your favorite?"

"Yes, it is, and this is a good one, but I make a better one from scratch at home."

"It looks really, really good," Blaze said suggestively while looking at Annabelle.

Annabelle nearly dropped the pie. She recovered just in time, holding the pie close to her chest with both hands now and still somehow holding on to the knife and plates.

Blaze scooted over. "Please, won't you join me for a quick dessert? I'd be so honored."

Blaze thought she was going to bolt back to the kitchen for a long moment, but then she put the pie down and slid into the booth, adjusting the hem of her floral print summer dress and crossing her legs at the ankles.

She smiled nervously.

He waited, enjoying her being uncomfortable.

Finally she began to cut the pie, a small piece for herself and a quarter of the pie for him. "It's not like me to be tongue-tied. You make me a little bit nervous."

"I'm sorry, Annabelle. How about I promise not to kiss you unexpectedly, at least until another day?" Blaze smiled as she stopped breathing again.

"I'm not sure that's helping at all!" She fanned herself with her napkin.

Blaze dug into the pie while she watched him eat. She took the tiniest of bites now and then while he cleaned his plate.

"So, I won't be in town but a few more days on this trip but I should be back in a few weeks. Maybe we could catch a movie or dinner real soon? Or, at least the next time I come through here?" Blaze realized he had started out just playing with her, but he really wanted her to accept his invitation.

"On one condition." Annabelle grinned at him.

"Just one?"

"Yes."

"What's that?" Blaze asked as he shifted just a little closer to her, fully expecting her to flirt with him in some fun southern way.

"You would have to pick me up at my house and come in and meet my mother for a few minutes."

"Well, that would be just fine, Annabelle." He liked saying her name. It suited her.

"Oh, you haven't met her yet."

"Whatever in the world do you mean?" Blaze asked. "Is she scary? Is she protective? Is she domineering? Is she judgmental?"

Annabelle sighed. "Yes," was all she said.

"Ok. I will happily do that."

"She also might not believe you exist if she didn't lay eyes on you for herself. I'll get you a box for the rest of the pie."

"Thanks. Can I ask a favor of you? Do you know if there's Uber, or a taxi in this town? I've got to get back out to the Stetson farm. I sent Mr Stetson on without me."

"You stayed here just to eat dessert with me?"

"I sure did. I don't mind admitting that." He could see her heartbeat in her throat.

"Aw, that's so sweet. Why don't you just take my car? Let me help you out. We'll figure out how to get it back to me later. I'll write my phone number on the box for the pie!" She took off before he had a chance to disagree.

Blaze watched her walk away and disappear behind the kitchen door. What was it about young southern women? This one had a walk you couldn't help noticing, and big sparkly eyes. He wanted to kiss her again and make her forget to breathe. He wanted to show her the world, at least for a while.

He realized he needed to find another reason to come to Kentucky soon.

She came back with her phone number written in a purple marker on the top of the box. There was even a heart drawn around it and her signature underneath. Her car keys laid on the top of the box.

"You've never even met me before. Are you sure you're ok with lending me your car?" Blaze stood up and took the box from her hands.

"I am a good judge of character, Mr Blaze Bangfield. Go on, now. It's the pale blue one. Just call me later." Her smile lit up the room.

Blaze thought about how many nice people there were in this area of the country all the way back to Glenwood's.

CHAPTER 33

*G*lenwood drove back to the farm thinking about Bruno. It still bothered him that they had to move the cows instead of Bruno himself. Maybe if Brody showed up later, the three of them could put enough pressure on Bruno to get him to cooperate. Cranky bulls could quickly become dangerous, but the animals would most always move away from the applied pressure.

That stubborn bull had dominance written all over him.

Glenwood might have to just give it up and try to sell him. He didn't like to keep things that were more trouble than they were worth.

He shut off the vehicle near the big barn and eased himself out of the truck. His right hip tended to lock up when he had been sitting in one position too long. He had sat on Paulo all morning, then driven to the Cowtown Diner, and back. Maybe he needed a good walk and some aspirin.

He was stretching his arms over his head to work the kinks out of his spine when he noticed movement in his peripheral vision. He barely had time to register the hairs standing up on the back of his neck when the angry snort of a bull came from way too close for comfort.

Glenwood went on high alert.

He started slowly turning toward the sound.

He barely had time to realize that this wasn't one of his bulls - *what in tarnation? Whose animal is loose in my driveway?* - when he knew he had to move away from the threatening bull.

He doubled up his fist to try to hit the bull in the middle of his head as he turned around, but it was too late. Suddenly he felt himself being thrown up and knocked down to the ground by the big animal. It knocked the wind completely out of him. Gravel tore at his arms.

Before he could even move, the angry bull lunged at Glenwood's body on the ground and threw him up higher into the air.

Glenwood felt the big horn go through his left side and the next thing he noticed, he was on the ground again between the barn and the truck.

Without a thought for his bleeding side, he crawled as fast as possible under the truck. He made it the three feet of distance and scooched as far as he could on his belly, with his left arm underneath his weight.

He thought this might help slow the blood pouring out of the wound where the bull had gored him.

Glenwood barely fit under there at all but was extremely grateful for the cover.

The bull! Where is he?

He could see the bull's legs right beside the truck and hear the snorting and bellowing sounds. This big boy, whoever he was, was still having a raging fit two feet away.

Ok, I'm still conscious. I'm safe under here for now. I think I might have two wounds and I am alone. It hurts like hell to breathe. Where is my phone?

He tried to move his right arm toward the back pocket of his jeans.

No phone.

The bull was still snorting and pawing the ground and Glenwood knew that adrenalin was helping him not feel too much pain, at least for now. He had a feeling it was going to be the worst pain ever, soon enough. He knew he had to remain calm.

If Glenwood Stetson got out of this predicament alive, he would never admit to anyone that he was scared to death.

I hope it's just a glancing blow. I don't seem to be bleeding out but I'm pretty sure I've got some broken ribs.

Blaze!

Blaze said he would be just a few minutes behind me.

CHAPTER 34

Savannah walked out to her car, holding her coffee. She appreciated the perfect summer weather for a nice drive toward home. She realized that her mood felt a lot sunnier, too, since deciding to go on home now, instead of tomorrow.

It seemed as if all the birds in town were singing, just to cheer her up and sing about how she needed to choose to be happier than she had been lately.

She tried to echo one of the bird's little tunes, and laughed aloud at how bad it sounded. Whistling was not one of her gifts.

Brody sure can sound just like all kinds of birds. Why, oh, why couldn't he just be all that I thought he was? Get over it, girl. Come on, now.

Savannah sat in her car and decided to call her dad before she headed home for her much-needed visit. She had no idea what he had planned for today. She didn't want to interrupt anything, so giving him a heads-up was only fair.

I'll tell him I'm coming today for a visit. I'll see if he needs me to pick anything up on the way. There's no telling how bad he's been eating with me gone!

She dialed the number and let it ring a long time.

When the voicemail picked up, she said, "Hey, daddy. You must be out at the barns or something. I just wanted to let you know I'm headed home for an overnight visit. We'll go to church in the morning, ok? Text me if you need me to pick up anything on the way. Love ya!"

Savannah set the phone down in the passenger seat and turned the country music up loud.

She put on her favorite sunglasses and headed home as the words to Brody's text played over and over in her mind.

"I have it all figured out. We must talk soon, face to face."

CHAPTER 35

*B*rody found the little coffee shop easily enough and drove past it. Savannah's car was not in the parking lot.

Next, he checked to see if she was parked anywhere in the blocks close by. No luck there either.

He decided a coffee would really hit the spot so he parked and put Chance on her leash, taking her with him.

He noticed the flowers he had bought were fading fast. *Maybe it's the thought that counts.*

If he found Savannah soon, the big bouquet might perk up in a tall vase with water. He felt like a man on a mission to keep things alive; this puppy, these flowers, and his wilted relationship with the girl he couldn't get out of his head.

Chance seemed thrilled to be going into the coffee shop, with all the new smells.

Brody ordered a large coffee for the road, and spoke to the guy at the counter. He wanted to ask him a question.

"Sure, buddy. A question about lattes?"

"No. I'm looking for a girl."

"Ok," the guy hesitated. "What's your type?" the guy went on playfully.

Brody pulled up a photo of Savannah on his phone. "Oh, sorry. A specific girl. This one."

The guy laughed. "Savannah. She was just here. I swear she just left, maybe ten minutes ago. Nice girl. Loves her coffee."

Brody threw his money down on the counter and scooped up the puppy and his coffee. "Thanks, mister! You just made my day."

"No problem. Cute dog. Good luck!"

Brody wanted to hurry back onto the road. He had to get back to Savannah's parking lot as fast as possible. He was finally going to explain everything to her. He would hold her in his arms, and make everything so much better!

Before he could leave, Chance took her own sweet time to go pee. Brody held onto his patience. Savannah was worth waiting for. It wouldn't be long now.

I can't wait to tell her it was all mistaken identity. She will see that she shouldn't have just taken off without even talking to me.

I'm nothing like my brother.

Savannah, I'm coming, little darling.

As he pulled back into the same parking space he had been in before, he wondered where she was now because she sure wasn't here. She hadn't come straight back from the coffee shop. Maybe she ran into the grocery or hit a drive-thru for some food.

It didn't matter. His plan was to wait.

He got out of the truck and made himself comfortable under the same tree. He gave Chance a puppy treat from his pocket and settled back. She swallowed the treat quickly and turned in a circle before flopping down on the grass right up against him.

He shifted his cowboy hat so he could lean against the tree more comfortably and began to echo the birds in the tree branches above him.

He wasn't moving from this spot until he saw the love of his life and finally had his chance to make things right again.

CHAPTER 36

Come on, Blaze! I'm going to need a little help making a 911 call. I sure don't want to bleed to death here under my truck.

By this time, Glenwood wondered how long he had laid underneath his vehicle. He tried to breathe shallowly and keep his wits about him.

The bull wasn't budging, either. He was still snorting and bellowing right beside the truck.

Glenwood heard a low growling from the other side of his vehicle. He saw black paws crouched beside him. Cinder!

The last thing in the world Glenwood wanted was for Cinder to get thrown up in the air and hurt by this bull, too.

"Cinder! No!"

Ow, it hurts to yell.

Cinder growled again from the opposite side of the truck and the bull seemed madder than ever, if that were possible.

"Cinder, be careful, buddy," Glenwood whispered.

Keep this bull engaged but keep the truck between you two. I'm going to feed you a ribeye steak when I get out of this mess. You are such a good boy.

Glenwood felt better because he didn't feel so alone in this situation, but he wondered just how long he could hang on. His side and belly felt sticky and wet.

He was so tired, even with the bull snorting and Cinder going back and forth and growling.

Then he remembered to pray.

Lord, I'm not here alone. Why, you've been with me all along. Please, Lord, help get me out of this. If it's not your will to keep me on this Earth a while longer, then please watch over Savannah. I don't want to leave my baby girl like this.

That's when he heard the approach of a car.

Thank you, Jesus!

CHAPTER 37

*I*t took a few moments for Blaze to move the seat back and adjust the steering wheel height in Annabelle's tiny pale blue car before he could fold himself into the driver's seat. He thought this car matched her perfectly, since it was so small and impractical.

Laughing at what Glenwood would think when he pulled up in this little baby car, Blaze enjoyed his drive back to the farm.

The most surprising thing about this trip to Kentucky was that he hadn't been bored here. He thought he would free-lance with his high-paying international client and immediately board a plane home to Montana, but he had very much enjoyed the company of a lovely redhead. He had flirted seriously with Annabelle and looked forward to working a few more hours with Glenwood this afternoon. Heck, he even had to admit it had been good to see his brother, at least for a while.

He had planned to give his brother a hard time, and then give him a check for a large portion of the buy-out. Maybe he was getting soft. Pushing Brody's buttons wasn't as much fun as it used to be.

He was in such a good mood, he even hoped Brody would get back before they were finished. He needed to talk to his brother about their father's ranch and then hand Brody a six-figure check to seal the deal. If Brody didn't want to own a ranch with Blaze, then Blaze would find the money and completely buy him out. It wouldn't take him long, either.

It seemed like Kentucky really was a very special place.

Maybe that's why he looked forward to getting Annabelle's car back to her.

He drove down the long winding driveway in the tiny car and beeped the high-pitched horn several times so that Glenwood would see the tiny car approaching if he was outside nearby.

Still laying on the horn, he came around the last corner of the driveway and hit the brakes hard.

What is going on here?

Someone's bull was on the loose and it was stomping mad.

It stood to the side of Glenwood's truck and turned enough to face the little car, pawing the ground and turning its head back and forth.

Blaze cracked a window and tried to run through some possibilities.

Where is Glenwood?

I'd hate to let this bull tear up Annabelle's car. She might have second thoughts about dinner with me.

Blaze heard growling and barking as Cinder came around to the bull's backside, giving the back legs plenty of room, but bothering him a lot. The bull jumped up in the air and came down sideways from where he had been. Cinder came right on up to the little car and gave several short barks while looking right at Blaze.

Blaze shut off the car.

"Cinder! Hold!"

Blaze listened for a moment but didn't hear anything but

the bull bellowing. That's when he noticed that Glenwood's driver side door was open.

He beeped the horn several times to keep the bull focused.

Cinder whined and kept pacing about three feet between Blaze's borrowed car and Glenwood's truck.

Blaze called out, "Glenwood? Glenwood!"

Faintly there came an answer. "I'm hurt. Call 911."

Oh, no.

Blaze saw legs underneath the truck. He pulled out his phone and hit the numbers.

911.

"I'm bleeding," Glenwood gasped.

"We've got this, Glenwood. Just breathe."

"Don't get out of that car," he choked out.

"911. What is your emergency?"

Blaze explained about the crazed bull on the loose and that Glenwood was hurt and under the truck.

"This bull has been in a tizzy for a while here. I'll keep Glenwood talking and try to figure out some kind of containment plan for the bull," Blaze said.

"Sir, we will send an officer also. The ambulance is enroute, about eight to ten minutes from you."

Blaze thought that sounded good, as far out in the country as they were. He told her she did not need to stay on the line with him and shut off his phone.

"Glenwood, you staying with me?" Blaze called out the window.

"Best I can," came the weak voice.

"They'll be here any second."

Then Blaze started up the car again. Every couple of minutes he inched forward. He hoped to distract the bull, or run it off before the ambulance got here. At the very least he would try to back the bull up some.

Maybe he should call Brody? No, Brody was off on some

secretive personal mission that involved romance. He might not even be anywhere near here. Blaze decided he would wait and call him after the EMTs got Glenwood settled into the ambulance.

The minutes ticked by slowly. Blaze felt so helpless and he didn't like that one bit. Cinder was laying down right beside Glenwood's truck and on alert to the movements and sounds of the bull.

Come on, guys. Come on.

He inched the bull a little farther away from the truck, hoping the massive animal would not try to gore Annabelle's cute little car. The bull bellowed and bucked in front of the car.

Maybe beeping this horn is not helping this bull at all. He sure doesn't want to back up any. He could probably flip this car over and then I'd be sharing the ambulance with Glenwood.

He shut off the car and took his hand off the horn, straining to try to hear a siren in the distance. Time was ticking by, and Blaze hated that he couldn't get out of the car and check on Glenwood, or help him in some way right now.

IN THE BLESSED silence the bull seemed to finally calm down some. He edged toward the open door of the truck, and away from the little car, sniffing and snorting at the opening.

The silence lengthened painfully.

Suddenly the screeching vocals and guitars of ACDC's Thunderstruck blasted from Glenwood's phone.

The bull jumped backward, startled, and then turned and trotted off over the hill and out of sight.

"Glenwood, I don't know whose ringtone that was but the bull didn't like it! He's clear out of sight. Glenwood?"

"My daughter."

Blaze eased himself out of the car and edged toward the rise in the hillside so he could keep his eyes on the bull.

. . .

A POLICE CAR roared up the long driveway and passed close to the passenger side of Annabelle's car. The ambulance, lights flashing, was right behind him.

Everyone quickly and cautiously got out of the vehicles and the emergency medical technicians began to work on getting Glenwood out from under the truck, stabilized, and into the ambulance.

The policeman headed toward Blaze who had kept an eye on the bull. Blaze filled him in and pointed out the big beast in the distance.

The bull was still heading toward the back road, walking along as if he had caused enough trouble in one place for today.

Since Blaze could guard against the bull in case he turned around, the policeman headed back to his cruiser to call animal control about the bull.

Blaze asked him if he knew Glenwood, and was there anyone they should call. He walked back over to the truck and picked up Glenwood's phone from the passenger seat.

"Yes. We'd better contact his daughter, Savannah."

"Officer, Mr Stetson's phone is right here. A crazy loud ringtone is what ran the bull off. ACDC. Thunderstruck."

"That might run me off, too," the officer laughed as he watched the EMT's load Glenwood into the back of the ambulance with practiced efficiency.

"I don't know his daughter. My brother's been working here. I could call him," Blaze said.

Officer Ford pulled out his phone. "My sister is Savannah's best friend. I got it," he said as he pulled up Lana's number. "You call your brother. You want to follow me to the hospital?"

"Yes, sir. I need to get this car back to town for -"

"Annabelle," they both said at the same time just as the

ambulance headed down the long tree-lined driveway toward the local hospital.

CHAPTER 38

*S*avannah stopped at a rest area for a quick bathroom break. She knew she'd had too much coffee. She got out of the car to stretch her legs and check her phone since she was way too smart to look at her phone while driving.

Oh, my gosh. A ton of phone messages and texts from Lana? What in the world?

Maybe she's still thinking up more things for us to do tomorrow?

There are times in your life where everything instantly changes; moments that will be remembered exactly as they happened because they carry such a turning point. This was one of those moments for Savannah. As she read through Lana's texts to hurry home, and asking why she wasn't answering her phone, Savannah realized she needed to get home fast. Her daddy was hurt! Luckily, she was already halfway there.

She said a grateful prayer and got right back in her car. The bathroom break was long forgotten as she heard the phone messages from Lana.

Lana said her brother, Creed, had called and told her to get ahold of Savannah. Mr Stetson was being taken to the hospital and that he was heading into surgery from being gored by a bull!

Lana also said she was heading there now, and not to worry.

Really, Lana? Don't worry? Oh, my gosh!

Daddy!

The messages had come in about 40 minutes ago. She called Lana as she got back onto the road.

It went to voicemail. She left a quick message.

"Oh, Lana, I was on my way home already when I stopped and saw your messages. I'll be at the hospital in under an hour. Don't worry. I'll be careful. See you there! Oh, and call me if anything changes."

Bruno! I'm going to kill him with my bare hands! Stupid bull.

How did this happen?

And if Brody had anything to do with it, he is going to hear from me, too! I wish I knew what happened.

Maybe I should call Brody.

No, just drive.

Why hasn't he called me about daddy?

Well, maybe he saved daddy's life.

I don't know. I don't know.

Oh, Brody, I'm so scared!

Dear Lord, watch over daddy and everyone who has anything to do with working on him or helping him. Thank you, too, that Creed knew Lana would call and text until she heard back from me.

Help me to drive safely and not too fast.

In Jesus' name, Amen.

CHAPTER 39

*E*very red light and stop sign had been excruciating as Savannah drove towards the hospital. She tried not to cry so hard that she couldn't see to drive. She tried to breathe slowly while she looked for a parking space in the Emergency parking lot. She tried not to run into the building.

She slowed to a walk.

She dug deep into her emotional strength as the harsh lighting and the overcrowded ER waiting room assaulted her senses. It seemed as if everything was in slow motion as she waited behind a man in front of her. He was asking about how long the receptionist thought they would have to continue waiting and that his wife was so sick and uncomfortable.

There were crying babies and a moaning old gentleman in a wheelchair. There were endless intercom interruptions that mixed together with the tv to form a discordant mixture of sounds. It all threatened to send her running from the room.

Her turn did finally come.

"I'll let Doctor Hudson know you're here. He'll want to talk to you as soon as he can." The girl in the cubicle seemed so calm.

Savannah found herself being sent to an inner waiting room

through the big double doors and down a long hallway where curtains were drawn around people with their beeping machines and quiet conversations.

How can everyone be so calm? Hurry up! I'm so scared and alone.

The inner waiting room was quieter and only held a few people. She was never as happy in her life to see Lana, who stood up and hugged her close.

"Lana, hey! What do we know?"

"Nothing. They aren't going to tell me anything, but I didn't want you waiting here alone. I'm so glad you got here safely."

The ER physician walked up and Savannah asked what he could tell her about her father, Glenwood Stetson.

"Your father is stabilized. X-rays show that his lungs are not collapsed but he does have some broken ribs. He's had a cat scan to check for internal injuries. It's being read now." The doctor took off his glasses and rubbed the bridge of his nose.

"Is he going to be ok?"

"He does have a good-sized flesh wound on his left side from the bull's horns. The general surgeon just got here. Hopefully all she will have to do in surgery is clean the wound and sew him up," said Dr Hudson.

"So, you're saying he's going to be ok?" Savannah asked.

"It looks that way. Mr Stetson was very lucky today. One of us will let you know how it's going."

Savannah could only nod her head. She was trembling and tears were pouring down her face. She let Lana thank the doctor and help her toward a chair.

She took a long shuddering sigh and looked up when the doors opened again.

The most handsome cowboy in the world walked in - her cowboy!

Brody!

Without letting herself think about it, she rushed across the waiting room and threw herself into his strong arms. She didn't care who was watching. She pulled his face down to hers and crushed him with a kiss; a kiss full of love and hope for the future, and a burning need to be -

He's not... wait a minute... this isn't right!

She threw her head back from his and searched his eyes, and what was up with this sly fox smile...

Why is he looking at me so strangely?

"I love when this happens! Brody is going to kill me," this handsome stranger laughed, holding her even tighter.

Savannah was mortified. "You're not Brody! Who are YOU?"

"I'm Blaze, Brody's identical twin," he said as he smiled down at her.

"Let me go right now. I don't want to have to head-butt you. Brody said he had an older brother." She struggled to get out of his embrace.

Blaze reluctantly let go of her and said, "Well, yes, by a couple of minutes, anyway."

Savannah looked from Blaze to Lana and back again. "I guess y'all have met?"

They both nodded and Lana rolled her eyes.

"So, I apologize for wrapping myself around you. You shouldn't have let me."

"Well, where's the fun in that?"

Blaze offered to get both girls a coffee when Savannah interrupted him.

"Yes, that'd be great, but wait a minute. Where IS Brody?"

She watched both Lana and Blaze look uncomfortable and Lana's eyes seemed round as golf balls.

"Oh, my gosh! I forgot to call Brody," Lana said as she pulled her phone out of the pocket of her hoodie.

"What?"

"Well, Blaze was working with your dad, and -"

"I never called him, either," said Blaze.

"I sure missed a lot when I left, huh?" Savannah cut in again.

"You sure did. Ok, Brody's at your little rental, waiting for YOU! He wanted to surprise you and explain everything! Oh, I'm so sorry, Savannah! When your dad got hurt, I forgot about him!" She stepped away to make the call, but looked back and said, "Brody's going to want that kiss for himself, you know!"

Blaze went to get the coffee, laughing at his own antics as he left.

As THE MINUTES slowly ticked by, Savannah had some friends of her dad's come by, to pray and to check on him. The older gentlemen sat together and figured out a schedule to help with feeding the cattle and other essential things. Savannah thanked them and mentioned that if they needed any other help, they could reach out to Leon, from the Young Farmers.

"Now, that's a good idea, Miss Savannah. I'll see to it that he gets in on the rotations. I know him. He's a fine boy, and don't you worry about anything with the farm. If you think of anything else, you just call me, now, you hear?" Old Mr Jones gave her a bear hug as his friends stood up to leave.

The pastor from Pleasant Hillside came next, praying with everyone in the waiting room who wanted to stand in a circle holding hands. Savannah noticed that Blaze hesitated, but then joined with the hands on either side, closing the circle.

I wish Brody could see this. I think he would be proud of his "older" brother. I think I'm glad he didn't see me throw myself into Blaze's arms and kiss him, though.

Brody! Hurry up and get here!

CHAPTER 40

Brody hoped he didn't have too much time to kill before Savannah showed up. He looped Chance's leash around the base of the tree and started warming up his upper body, swinging his arms. He stopped long enough to take his shirt off and put it in the seat of the truck.

He hefted two five gallon water bottles out of the back of his truck. They were filled to the lids and were the kind with easy grip handles on the side. He started walking the perimeter of the parking lot, gripping the big blue bottles in each hand and concentrating on his shoulders and upper back.

Farmer carries. That'll make the time go by fast. Haha.

He spoke to Chance on every round when he got close to her. She always got up and wagged her tail and flopped her ears around. He threw in a few walking lunges for good measure on all the corners.

Savannah is going to love you, puppy. Eventually.

Round and around he went until his grip was about to give out. Then he put the water bottles back and cooled off, giving himself and Chance a drink of water before he put his shirt back on and joined his puppy under the tree again.

. . .

A SLIGHT BREEZE blew up from somewhere off to the east and it felt good to them both as they sat in the shade under the mighty white oak tree. He nodded off while imagining Savannah on horseback on a Sunday in the fall, surrounded by orange and gold leaves falling from the trees along the lower Bourbon Creek.

BRODY WOKE up to the ringing of his phone, covered in sweat, with a big furry puppy in his lap. It took him a moment to remember where he was - under the big tree and waiting for Savannah. Wow, July in Kentucky was hotter than blue blazes.

It was Lana.

"Hey, Lana. What's up?"

"It's not good, Brody, but don't freak out. Savannah's dad is in surgery here at the hospital."

"Oh, no! What happened? I've got to find Savannah! I'll find her!"

"No. Listen. She is right here in the waiting room with me. Get your cute butt back here, ok?"

"Ok, bye! Wait! Thanks, Lana."

"No problem, Brody. Be careful."

As luck would have it, Chance was peeing beside the tree they had been asleep under. Brody scooped her up and ran for his truck.

As he headed towards the main road, he realized he didn't ask why Glenwood was in surgery, but it must have been some sort of emergency. Well, he was needed there immediately, for Glenwood and Savannah.

He realized he needed to take the puppy by the bunkhouse before he would be able to go to the hospital. It was way too hot to leave her in the truck in the parking lot. It would take him a little longer to get there, but it could not be helped.

Chance could wait for him in the laundry room with food and water. There was a dog bed already in there.

Plans in place, and praying all the while, he drove back home.

Home is where the heart is, and Bourbon Creek was his home.

CHAPTER 41

*T*he waiting room was like a place where time stood still.

Savannah sat scrunched over in her seat while Lana showed her a funny cat video on youtube. Blaze was on his phone, too, on the other side of her. Bobby Joe had come straight from work to wait with Lana and had brought a dozen assorted donuts, but he couldn't get Savannah or Lana to even taste one.

"Oh, come on, girls, I picked these out for you two. You can't expect me to eat a dozen donuts by myself?"

Lana smiled at him. "I've seen you do it before, darling."

The automatic doors opened and took their attention away from long johns and sprinkled cake donuts with pink frosting.

"Family of Glenwood Stetson?" The general surgeon approached the group of people sitting in the waiting area. Everyone looked up at her with hopeful expressions on their faces.

Savannah waved awkwardly and stood up. "I'm his daughter."

"The surgery went well. We thoroughly cleaned your father's wounds and sewed him up. There were two of them, one much larger than the other. He didn't have to have a chest tube. The CT scan showed no internal damage."

Savannah tried to memorize every word this woman said. "So, that's good, right?"

The surgeon smiled. "Yes, very good. He will be moved to recovery soon and when he wakes up, we'll let you go back there and see him."

"Oh, thank you so much. He's going to be ok?"

"I do think so. We will keep him here at the hospital a couple of days for observation. He's on antibiotics and those ribs are going to give him grief every time he moves. Will he have help at home for a while?"

"Yes," said Savannah. "I'll be right there for whatever he needs. How long will the stitches be in place?"

"Two to four weeks. We will want to see him back in a week and we'll take it from there." She smiled at Savannah.

"Thank you so much."

"You're very welcome, dear."

SAVANNAH FELT relief flow through her veins and make another round. She suddenly felt like every bit of energy she had was expended from worrying, and praying, and all the long wait. She started hugging people, just so she wouldn't fall down to the floor. She reached for Lana and pulled her up out of her chair for a long hug.

"Thanks again for being here with me," she said.

"You would have done it for me." Lana sat down and gestured to Bobby Joe. "Stand up and hug that girl!"

Bobby Joe's hug was a bear hug and it gave Savannah strength. She laughed through her happy tears. He lifted her up off the ground and then let her go.

She turned to Blaze, who had already stood up and knew that he was the next hug.

She laughed as she hugged Blaze because this time it didn't seem weird at all to be in his arms for just a few seconds. She was just so happy about her daddy's -

"Savannah?"

Savannah jumped backwards out of Blaze's embrace and turned to look into Brody's eyes. He looked shocked and angry.

"Brody! Daddy's out of surgery and -"

Brody looked from his brother to Savannah. "So, you jump into my brother's arms, to celebrate?"

Savannah frowned at him. "No, wait a minute. You weren't here..."

Brody took one step closer to her. "Well, I'm here now!"

"Well, I'm here now, too!" She practically yelled right back at him, taking one step closer to him. Her heart was pounding clear out of her chest.

"So, we are both here now," he said.

Lana and Bobby Joe looked from one to the other, holding hands and hoping for the best.

"Ugh, I was so mad at you! Don't you know how mad you made me?" She seemed to have forgotten where she was, and that her voice should not be loud.

"Ugh, you wouldn't even talk to me! How was I supposed to explain anything?" He, too, was practically shouting.

"I saw you with some gorgeous redhead!"

"NO, you didn't. You saw HIM with a gorgeous redhead!"

"I was too mad to talk to you! That's just how I am," she said.

"But, you ran! We could have worked it out sooner!"

She watched him move closer again. "Well, we will have to just work it out right now!"

She threw herself into his arms so hard she nearly knocked him off his feet.

She kissed him with waves of anger, and energy, and happiness. She could immediately feel his longing for her. She clung to him as his kiss deepened, making her heart sing a new song while tears streamed down her face.

She couldn't seem to get her body close enough to his, from her mouth all the way down to her cowboy boots. Brody Bangfield was in her arms, and she was never letting go again. Never.

"Well, I'm about to get embarrassed here," Bobby Joe said as he cleared his throat loudly.

Savannah startled, suddenly remembered where she was. She felt Brody come back to reality, too, as he stopped kissing her and looked over at him.

"Oh, what'd you have to stop them for? I was getting a kick out of watching that." Blaze grinned.

Lana laughed at them both. "Y'all can get a room or something later. Sit down here and let's catch Brody up on what's been happening."

Brody and Savannah, blushing, held onto each other's hands and sat down as Blaze began to tell about the day's crazy events. "I can't tell you the part where the bull gored your father, Savannah. I wasn't there for that."

"I'm going to kill that Bruno when I see him. I don't know what he would bring in a sale, but I may just have to shoot him!" Savannah seethed.

"Hold on there, little filly. It wasn't Bruno. It wasn't any of your father's bulls. It was a young bull loose in your driveway," Blaze explained.

"Oh, my heck!"

Do we know where he came from?" Brody asked.

Bobby Joe leaned forward. "Some of the men from your church were here earlier. They think it was most likely Mizz Myrtle's. You know how bad most of her fencing is. They were headed over to feed your cattle and see if they could find out anything."

Blaze turned the conversation back towards the afternoon.

"So, anyway, I was pulling down the long driveway in Annabelle's little baby blue car and -"

"Wait," said Savannah. "Annabelle Burton? I'm so confused."

"Better stick around from now on," Brody teased.

"I think you can convince me, ok?" Savannah teased back as she squeezed his thigh.

Blaze, enjoying the attention, went on to tell about the frightening events, from when he saw Mr Stetson crammed up under his truck to how he couldn't get the bull to back off or calm down. He explained his frustration in knowing that Mr Stetson was bleeding and hurt and all he could do was wait for the emergency medical team.

Savannah nearly broke down again. "So, we don't know how long he was hurt, under there, scared and alone, except for Cinder. How could I have been so selfish to leave him? It's all my fault."

"It is not your fault at all," said Lana.

"I think you might have been the one to save him, Savannah. What's your dad's ringtone when you call him?" Blaze asked.

"Thunderstruck, ACDC. Why?"

"Well, when I stopped blowing the horn and it was finally quiet, the bull went over to the driver's side door. It was open, and Mr Stetson's phone was laying on the seat. That's when that song starting blasting loud. Like nails on a chalkboard. That's what startled the bull. He just took off over the hill after that."

Brody looked at Savannah, who had both hands on her temples, as if she were thinking hard. "You called him, didn't you?"

"I did! He didn't answer," she said.

"That's because he couldn't reach his phone from underneath his truck," Blaze explained. "So, see? It's not all your fault, at all."

Brody placed his hand on Savannah's leg and said, "You saved him. Your phone call ran off that crazed bull."

"Exactly," said Blaze.

Savannah looked around the room, blinking back tears again. She was so emotional after everything they had been through. "I guess I did help. Wow."

She looked over at Lana. "Remember when I talked him into using that ringtone for when I called? I love that song, and he said it was so annoying, he guessed it could work as my ringtone!"

Lana smiled. "Yeah, that was what, middle school? Crazy."

Bobby Joe and Lana got up to leave then. They said they both had early work schedules the next day and would check on her and her dad after work. They convinced Blaze that it would be no trouble to follow him to the Cowtown Diner so he could return Annabelle's car. Then, they could take him out to the farm so he could get his wheels and head back to his hotel.

Savannah could tell that they were trying to give her and Brody a little time alone. She really appreciated that. Lana was such a romantic.

Her friend hugged her one more time and then hugged Brody, too. "You can tell her about the puppy, now. Where is it, anyway? You need for us to take it home a day or two?"

"Puppy? I can't believe how much I missed!" Savannah turned to Brody with her full attention.

"No, thanks, Lana. She's in the laundry room at the bunkhouse. I'll go check on her soon. Bye, guys."

Savannah wanted to say a lot of things to Brody, now that they were alone in the waiting room. She paused, trying to decide how best to begin.

Brody beat her to it. "I had this whole idea about coming to see you. I was planning to sweep you off your feet earlier today. I was so lonesome without you around, like there was a hole in my chest the size of Montana. So, I looked at puppies over at Malachi Ford's place, and picked one out. Her name is Chance."

Savannah loved watching him. His face lit up as he talked about his new puppy. "When did you do this?" she asked.

He had to think for a minute. "This morning."

"You've had a really long day, too," she said.

"Wow. I sure have. You should have seen the workout I did in your parking lot there with two five-gallon water bottles."

"Ha! I bet the neighbors loved that." She could just imagine those ladies all peeking around the curtains at their windows!

"Anyway," he went on. "You're going to love this puppy and her crazy ears. I brought you a big bouquet of flowers with a huge bow, and I had the girl make a big bow for Chance's collar, too."

Savannah was touched by these details. She was a lucky woman, she realized, in more ways than one.

"So, where are my flowers?"

"They are laying on the seat of my truck and look pitiful since it's been so hot today. Chance tried to nibble in them, too. I'm sorry."

"No. Don't be sorry. That is a beautiful gesture, and I want the bow, anyway. Hey, Brody?"

"What?"

Savannah sighed. "I'm sorry. When I saw your identical twin, and thought it was you, some kind of switch clicked over in my brain, and I was so hurt and so mad. I realized how crazy I was about you because you could hurt me so much. That's what was wrong with me all day at the Young Farmers Day, and then I just took off the next morning. I mean it. I'm so sorry. You're right. We should have talked. Or, yelled, or something."

"Oh, it's been the longest two weeks without you around. We are going to be ok now, little darling." She noticed a sudden husky depth to his voice.

"I know. I didn't like thinking you were a big liar," she giggled.

. . .

THE NURSE CAME to take Savannah to the recovery room. "He's starting to wake up. Wanna' come on back for a little while?"

Savannah looked back at Brody.

"You go on, now," he said. "I'll be right here when you come back."

Savannah followed the nurse into a brightly lit room with many beeping machines and rhythmic sounds. She looked down at Glenwood Stetson, laying in the bed with his eyes closed. She reached out to hold the hand that didn't have the iv fluids going.

He looked so tired, older, and smaller, somehow. She had never seen him like this, and it was a lot to take in. Even when he napped on the couch in the den, he was a big presence in the room. This was different, and she had to admit that facing her father's mortality was a very scary thing. She never thought anything would ever happen to him.

Another nurse came in and introduced himself. "Let me grab a chair for you. Do you want something to drink?"

"No, I'm fine, thanks," she said, although her voice didn't sound fine at all. She sat down and continued to hold her father's hand. She began to talk to him about trivial things, just to pass the time. When she got around to saying that she was home for good this time, he slowly opened his eyes and swallowed painfully, but didn't say anything.

"Daddy? Hi, daddy." Tears dripped off her face and onto his warmed white blanket. Savannah wasn't sure her heart could hold this much gratitude.

Thank you, Lord God. Thank you. Bless all the people that have helped my daddy today.

The doctor came in some time later.

"Ok, he's doing a good job here. We're going to get him up in a room. He'll be on intravenous antibiotics for twenty-four hours. We're going to keep him overnight, maybe two nights. Starting tomorrow, he will need to do deep breathing exercises to decrease the chance of pneumonia. It's going to hurt like hell, since he has those broken ribs, but I'm sure you can encourage him to take it all seriously."

"Of course. Whatever he needs me to do," Savannah nodded, mentally making a list of things to help her father with to speed his recovery.

"Mr Stetson, you'd better listen to your daughter. I'm quite sure you will be the perfect patient." The doctor straightened up after looking into his eyes as if hypnotizing him.

Savannah sat while the doctor left and the nurse checked on him now and then, pushing injections of painkillers into his iv, and checking all the data.

"Ok, we're going to get him moved to a private room on level three. If you want to get your things, and your cowboy, you can follow him up." The nurse grinned at her as he left to check on his other patients.

CHAPTER 42

*I*t was well past visiting hours and Savannah could feel how tired she was deep in her bones. She had given her daddy many drinks of water. She had learned to encourage him to use the breathing exerciser as he would struggle to keep the little blue ball in midair for a moment or two. You could tell how much it hurt him, but he was tough as nails. "I don't want pneumonia on top of all this," he had said.

She looked over at Brody. He was dozing off in the chair in the corner with his long legs stretched out toward her. He had said he would stay if she would let him. He had gone to get her socks and bought her a sweatshirt because the room was so cold.

Brody really is the real deal. He wasn't full of lies. He wasn't at a concert with a gorgeous redhead. He really was with daddy, and then went to bed with his Kindle!

I wonder what he likes to read.

I can't wait to meet the puppy.

How could my life change so much in just one day?

How can I not jump to the wrong conclusions in my future? God in

Heaven, you will need to help me with this one! I want to be a better person.

The nurse finished with her hourly round and turned toward Savannah. "Mr Stetson will be resting as comfortably as possible for a few hours now. It might be a good time for you to go home and get some rest and freshen up. We can call you if there is any change at all." The nurse was the daughter of some friends from church and she smiled at Savannah encouragingly.

Brody looked up. "Let me drive you out to the farm, ok? We'll grab something to eat on the way. You really need to eat something."

Savannah wanted to resist their good advice.

The nurse waited for Savannah to listen to reason.

Glenwood groaned and held up his hand.

Savannah rushed back over to him and took his hand. "What is it, daddy?"

"I'll sleep until they wake me up to check on things, girl. Go on home a little while." He closed his eyes and took as deep a breath as he could.

Brody watched her lean over the bed railing and kiss her father on the cheek.

"I don't think I should leave your side. What can we do to make you feel better?" Savannah pulled his pillow straighter.

"Go home and make me some grandbabies," Glenwood said as he closed his eyes.

Savannah froze, wondering if Brody and the nurse heard him.

The nurse had heard him. She laughed and said, "Savannah, his meds will make him woozy, and he might say about anything right now. Looks like he's already asleep."

She really was feeling the exhaustion of all that had happened on this day. "Ok. You win, but we'll be right back."

CHAPTER 43

*B*rody and Savannah walked hand in hand down the
long halls of the local hospital and out to the visitor's
parking area. He led her to his truck. "Let's leave your car here."

He could hardly believe all the things that had happened in
such a short amount of time. He knew God was giving him a
chance to take care of his girl, though, and she was absolutely
worn out emotionally.

He watched her pick up the big bouquet of flowers on the
seat before she climbed up and held them in her lap.

"Those flowers look mighty pitiful by now," he laughed.

"Well, they mean the world to me. Some of them might even
perk up at home when I get them in water. Thank you."

He took his right hand off the steering wheel and reached
out to squeeze her hand.

She was about to doze off already. "I thought you were too
tired to drive safely yourself," he whispered.

She caught a cat nap as he drove to find some fast food.

He ran through a drive-through and folded down the paper
of a beef burrito with guacamole. "Here," he said as he handed it
to her.

"Ugh."

"You're hungry and tired and stressed. Come on. Try to eat a little." He took a huge bite of his burrito and pulled back onto the road.

He tried not to worry about how quiet she was on the drive back. He prayed silently that he could remember Glenwood's advice, to give her time. He prayed that she would start talking. He thanked God above that he was actually with Savannah again, even under these awful circumstances.

Then he prayed for Glenwood and for all the hospital staff.

He drove down the long driveway in the dark silence and headed toward the main house.

It was strange to see Glenwood's truck sitting by the barn. Brody's mind imagined being gored by a bull and then taking shelter underneath. He forced his mind away from those thoughts and focused on Savannah.

Finally she spoke. "Brody, is it ok if we go to the bunkhouse? I don't want to be in the house when daddy's in the hospital. No, wait. I guess I would be ok if you stay with me at the main house. I don't know. Decisions are too much for me right now. I just don't want to be alone right now."

"Sure thing, little darling." He could see how hard she had been trying to keep it together and there wasn't much left by now. She had forgotten all about his puppy. He would sneak down in a little bit and take care of Chance.

He led her into the main house and onto the couch. "You want a cup of tea?"

"No, I'd like to take a shower and I guess try to get a couple of hours of sleep. You know I can't be gone long. I feel like I need to be there right now."

"I know. It's so hard to get any rest in a hospital room with everything going on. We aren't far from there if they call. Want me to turn the water on for you and grab you a pair of your sweatpants and a shirt?"

"That would be perfect."

He jumped up from the couch and headed down the hall.

"Upstairs," she said.

WHILE SHE WAS in the shower, he ran to take Chance out and give her a little attention.

He hadn't been back long when she came back to the couch, her hair smelling faintly of strawberries. He had never seen her when her hair was wet. Gorgeous.

A roaring tidal wave of longing for her hit him. It was getting harder to hold back his love for her. He waited for the passionate feelings to subside. He reminded himself that she was exhausted from driving back to town and being so worried about her father during his surgery.

It's not every day that your dad gets gored by a bull and lives to tell the tale!

She cuddled up against him on the couch and promptly fell asleep.

He let himself reach over and smell her hair as he grabbed the blanket on the back of the couch. He covered her legs and feet.

He was happy that she felt safe in his arms and he counted his blessings, like sheep, until he dozed off, too.

IT WAS ALMOST sunrise when Brody woke almost three hours later. He eased his arm out from under Savannah and headed to the kitchen to make coffee, checking his phone as he walked.

He ran down to the bunkhouse to walk Chance and to feed her.

"I'm sorry, little fluff ball. I hate to leave you alone when I just got you, but I'll be back real soon. I promise." Chance seemed happy with that.

As he came back into the main house he heard Savannah stirring around so he poured their coffee.

"Let's watch the sunrise on the porch before we head back into town," she said as she took her steaming mug. She held the blanket around her shoulders.

They drank their coffee and snuggled together while the sky lit up with all the many colors of a very special sunrise.

"Yesterday was the longest day in my whole life," she whispered as she drank the coffee as it cooled down.

"So many ups and downs," he whispered back.

"When I think about how close we came to losing daddy, and you weren't here, and I wasn't here," Savannah's voice choked on the emotions running through her. "We should have been here, together."

Brody caught the tear that ran down her cheek with his thumb. "None of us have a guarantee on tomorrow, little darling. That's why we thank the Lord for every day. We just have to make the very best of it we can, together."

She smiled. "Together."

He watched her sipping his coffee, since hers was empty, as she looked out over the rolling hills of the land they both loved now.

His heart was here, in Kentucky, with Savannah and her people.

Suddenly the sharp percussion sounds from a woodpecker reached them. Brody held his breath, wondering if she was remembering when she had driven away from him.

"I've always loved the sounds of woodpeckers working so hard, until the last few weeks," she said.

The sounds came again from a different place.

Brody noticed her looking at him and reached over and hugged his woman even closer as he said, "Some people think hearing a woodpecker is a lucky sound. It stands for the rhythms of life. It can also mean change is coming. Digging into the tree is like digging into your own life to find solutions."

"I've heard that before. Some people around here say woodpeckers stand for seeing things in black and white. The red on their heads stands for defending what you hold most dear," she said.

"Savannah, I hold you most dear," he said, and his voice cracked with emotion.

"Hey, I'll say it first. I love you, Brody. I hold you most dear, too."

He thought his life could never be happier than this moment. He brought her hand to his heart.

"I want you to know that I plan to ask you to marry me. I just don't have a ring yet or anything. But, Savannah, you surely know by now that I want to spend the rest of my days with you, if you will let me," he said.

He started to lean over to kiss her thoroughly but she beat him to it.

The passion between them kicked up so suddenly that neither of them could breathe. It was like a sudden summer storm of emotions.

"I love you, Savannah."

He pulled her over onto his lap. They kissed for their second chance at love. They kissed for the fear of not knowing what would happen in the future.

He felt so lost as she pulled her head back from him.

She ran the back of her hand across her mouth. "Wow," she said. "I'm glad I called the hospital and checked on daddy before we came out here with our coffee. So... since we are planning to get married... can we get married as soon as daddy can get up and walk me down the aisle?"

Brody suddenly knew a deeper peace than he could have ever imagined. This straight-shooting woman of his... of HIS!

"Yes! As soon as you can plan a wedding like you want."

"Ok. And one more thing. Brody, can we start the honey-moon early, like before we go back over to the hospital? Please?" She put his coffee cup down.

Brody picked her up, quilt and all, and headed back into the house as fast as he could manage.

CHAPTER 44

*G*lenwood had had a long night of sleeping in short sections in between getting bothered by nurses and people who wanted to take blood constantly. They made him get up and go to the bathroom. They made him do his torturous breathing exercises. They made him drink broth and jello.

"That is not food. I hope someone brings me a decent steak later today," he grumbled.

He couldn't wait to be able to go home. He hoped to have a quiet day and prayed that they would all stop poking and prodding him so much. It was exhausting.

Promptly at 9am when visiting hours began, Glenwood heard the clip-clopping of high heels coming into his room. That did not sound like Savannah.

He painfully adjusted himself in the bed and looked toward the door just as Beulah Burton came bursting into the room. She wafted a cloud of rose perfume and wore a print dress with bright pink roses the size of dinner plates.

She picked up the remote for the tv and turned it off.

"Glenwood, oh no, I just heard about your accident! I came

over as soon as I fixed my hair. How are you feeling this morning?"

He watched her pat her stiffly sprayed hair.

She placed her pink and teal purse on the chair and came closer. As she fluffed his pillows, she leaned in and kissed him on the cheek, leaving a bright pink imprint of her lips.

"Here now, Beulah. You don't need to be doing all that. I am going to be fine in no time at all."

"Maybe it is time for you to let me take care of you."

"I don't need to be taken care of -"

"Says the man in the hospital bed!"

"Ok, it was nice of you to drop by."

"Well, I have already called my prayer group and asked them to put you at the top of our prayer-chain list. Will they let you eat solid food yet?" She patted his leg and went on without giving him time to answer. "I've already run by CowTown and left perfect directions for your favorite burger, just the way you like it. As soon as they open, someone's gonna' run you some decent food over here! Why, a man can't get his strength back on hospital liquids. I've got everything under control, so all you have to do is rest."

"I was just complaining about food restrictions." Saying this made him cough a little, and it hurt so bad he tried not to cough again.

"Oh, it just breaks my heart to see you in pain, Glenwood. Is Savannah here somewhere? Listen, if she needs a break, all you have to do is let me know, and I'll come sit here with you any time at all, day or night."

"She'll be here any minute, but that's very neighborly of you," he said. He wished she wouldn't try to be so helpful.

Beulah started straightening the room up. She briskly folded a blanket at the foot of the bed, and gave him a drink of water. She picked up the cafeteria menu and got a pink and teal striped pen out of her purse. She pulled the chair up very close and crossed her legs, looking up at him to see if he had noticed.

"I might as well help you fill out your meal requests on this menu, ok? Now, would you like scrambled eggs and toast in the morning or oatmeal with raisins? I think the protein would do you the most good, so I'm going to go ahead and check that. Ok."

He watched her check off the items on both sides, reading them aloud to him and marking what she thought was best. Her bracelets clanked on the wooden arm rest of the chair as she finished up.

Glenwood dozed off and on through most of that. He couldn't very well escape her while in a hospital bed.

He awoke a while later, to see that Beulah was still sitting beside him. She was reading a paperback book, sitting up straight and tall. The book was titled The Power of a Praying Wife.

Lord, have mercy. She doesn't have a subtle bone in her body.

"Beulah, if your perfume makes me sneeze, it's going to hurt my broken ribs."

"Oh! Well, I won't wear any when I come back this afternoon."

Savannah and Brody quietly entered the room.

"Thank goodness," Glenwood said, giving Savannah a look that said volumes.

He watched Savannah approach. She sure looked happy this morning and it did him good to see that.

She came on the other side of the bed and grinned at him in a funny way as she held his hand. "I see you have company already this morning."

Beulah stood up and picked up her purse. "Hello, Savannah. Now that you are here, where you should be, I'll be going on about my business. I filled out your father's cafeteria choices for him and I'm having his favorite lunch sent over from the diner in a couple of hours. So, you don't have to worry about that. Glenwood said he was so hungry." She turned back to the patient. "If you need anything else, now, you just call me. I'll check in on you later."

She gave Glenwood's leg a squeeze and clip-clopped out of the room.

Glenwood wondered why Savannah laughed as she reached out and patted his leg, too. Then she looked at him and said, "All the kissing!"

This comment made Brody laugh, too.

"What in tarnation is so funny?" Glenwood wanted to know. "I didn't ask her to visit me."

"Did you ask her to kiss you?"

"What? No. Of course not."

Glenwood's daughter pulled out her phone and took a photo of his face and then turned her phone around.

He looked at the bright pink lip marks on his cheek. Then, he held still while his daughter wiped off the traces of lipstick that Beulah Burton had left there on his face.

"That woman," he said.

CHAPTER 45

Savannah looked up as Brody came down the hospital corridor carrying a caramel latte from the cafeteria. Her cheeks warmed as memories from earlier that morning ran through her head. He was just so handsome and solid.

"What's up?"

"They took him down for a chest x-ray to make sure his lungs were inflated. They're getting him back in bed now."

She could hear her father moan as he was being helped into the bed. The sound tore through her heart.

"He is going to be ok. We can handle this. We'll figure everything out."

She felt so lucky to have him here to encourage her.

"I know. Thanks." She reached up for a quick kiss and took his hand.

They went in together as soon as the transport people came out.

Glenwood looked tired, but better. Savannah pulled a chair close.

"Shew, that wore me out," he said.

"You just rest now and they might let you go home tomorrow," Brody said. He was sitting on the windowsill between flowers from Pleasant Hillside church and the Kentucky Young Farmers group.

"The doctor said we might not know how much damage has been done to me for six months," he said to Brody. "I don't want to be down that long. I will lose my everloving mind."

"Your job right now is to think positive," Brody said. "You tell me what to do and I'll see that it all gets done. Savannah can put it all in her planner."

Savannah sipped her latte and sighed in happiness. "Daddy, I will never forget the look you gave me when the doctor said your belly fat might have saved you from a worse injury!"

"Don't make me laugh. It hurts too much."

"Well, you've got to admit it was funny," she said.

"So, no more fussing at me about what I eat?"

"I can't promise you that. I love you and want you to be healthy."

She helped her daddy do his deep breathing exercises. She could tell how painful they were. "Good job, daddy! Your lungs are as tough as nails. We've got to get you up and out of here as soon as possible..."

She shot Brody a questioning look and he nodded back. "I mean, we've got an engagement party to plan, and then a wedding," she went on.

Glenwood reached for his ice water.

Savannah could see her words sink into his tired mind.

"You two have decided to get married?" he asked. "And then, grandbabies?" He seemed to perk up a little.

Savannah laughed. "Probably."

She looked over to see how Brody was handling this, but his look was supportive, to say the least.

"Well, I can't think of a better reason to get well." He barely got the words out before he dozed off, with a smile on his face.

$\mathcal{T}$he cool wind running through the tops of the trees pulled Brody's attention away from the puppy rolling around at his feet. It felt like the weather was about to change as the trees swayed back and forth. He hoped this dog wouldn't tremble when thunder and lightning came rolling in across the fields. He'd owned dogs like that before and always felt bad for them.

"Chance, girl, things are looking up. Cinder, don't you agree?"

The dogs barely noticed him.

He'd left Savannah at the hospital with Glenwood. She was in her element, catering to her dad's every need and fielding how long all his visitors stayed. She had been in such a good mood. It did his heart good to think that he was a part of the reason for that.

Chance was playing with Cinder, trying to act like she was so tough. Cinder seemed happy to have her wallering all over him and pretending to growl.

As Blaze pulled down the long drive, Brody wondered why he had called and asked if he could come to talk to him. Well, better here than at the hospital, just in case they became annoyed with each other. He swore he would try to have great patience.

Maybe he's leaving now. He's probably got better things to do than try to make my future father-in-law like him more than he likes me.

Cinder stood at attention and watched Blaze get out of his truck. Chance got up and stood on the other side of Brody, mimicking the older dog. Brody patted them both.

"Good dogs."

The brothers greeted each other and walked into the bunkhouse den.

"So, how's Glenwood?"

"He is a tough old bird. They said they might let him go home tonight, or no later than in the morning."

Blaze stretched his legs and put his gleaming cowboy boots up on the coffee table. "I'm glad to hear that. After what we went through together, I feel pretty close to him. Seems like you've found yourself a great little setup here."

What does he mean by that? Oh, come on, Brody, give your big brother the benefit of the doubt.

"Well, Blaze, so far, so good. You won't have to be worrying about me coming back to Montana and dad's ranch. I'm in love with Savannah and I'm staying here."

Brody warily watched his twin brother laugh heartily.

"Well, after the way she threw herself into my arms and kissed me in the waiting room, I can't blame you one bit for that decision. She is a beauty. To be fair, though, she thought it was you."

Brody decided not to rise to the bait. He just nodded and said, "Thank you. We are going to get married. Soon."

Blaze went on. "Congratulations! I can tell that she'll never get us mixed up again."

"Well, I hope not." Brody found himself grinning.

"Listen, I've got to fly out of here later today, so I had to come out and talk to you, little brother. You left Montana all in a huff and I let you hang on to misunderstandings completely on purpose. That was fun, then, but it wasn't right of me."

Brody had no clue where this was going but it sounded like some sort of apology. "Explain." He still felt on guard.

Blaze took a long breath. "Dad never said he was leaving me the ranch. He said we would never be able to run the ranch together, yes, but he also said that I should buy you out. I just didn't tell you that part. I've always enjoyed watching you squirm and get mad and try not to act mad."

"You sure have. But, why hasn't dad told me that?"

Blaze laughed. "Oh, he said we would work it out sometime down the road. So, it's time to do that, Brody. I've been busting my chops throwing money together and I have a check for you right here. It's not for half the place, yet, but I should get the rest of it to you within a couple of years."

He held a check out to Brody.

Brody's eyes widened at the amount written there in thick black ink.

"Ok. Wow." He looked at his brother. "This will sure help me and Savannah get off to a good start in our life together."

"It ought to! So, if you agree, I'll have the paperwork drawn up and sent to you, along with copies of the appraisals."

"Blaze, this is incredible. Does this amount strap you for cash?" Brody was still staring at the check.

"Of course not. I'm not that nice! Now, when is this wedding? I really don't want to miss it."

"I'll let you know, and Blaze, I really want you to be there. You seem, I don't know, different. I really like it." Brody grinned at his brother, knowing he probably sounded silly.

He pulled his brother close for a quick hug as they stood up.

"Well, now and then, I try to be a better man. One of these days, I think it'll stick," Blaze laughed.

Brody heard a car pulling down the driveway. As he went to

the window, he said, "Savannah says the wedding should be as soon as Glenwood can walk her down the aisle."

"Well, you surely have enough sense to give that woman what she wants!"

There was a loud knock on the door. Brody opened it to a man in uniform who looked from one twin to the other and said, "Which one of you do I know already?"

"Me," Blaze said.

"Come on in," Brody opened the door wider. "I'm Brody Bangfield. You already know Blaze."

"Yes. Officer Ford here. You can call me Creed. I'm Lana's brother."

Brody shook his hand, looking for a resemblance, and the men all sat down.

"Well, I met your other brother just a few days ago," Brody said.

Creed Ford smiled. "Which one? Malachi?"

"Yes. Did the puppy out there give it away?" Brody asked.

"Sure did. I just left the hospital. I talked to Glenwood and he sent me here to fill you in. When Glenwood was hurt, we found out that the bull on the loose belonged to Mizz Myrtle."

"Really? I've been trying to help her out with her fencing when I'm down that way," Brody said.

"Oh, I like hearing that. Anyway, she walked out and showed me her fence lines were down. Every single bit of fencing that backs up to the property here was down. Somebody cut it all."

"What? That's mighty suspicious."

"Oh, yeah. Easy to see it was on purpose. We're looking into it, especially since Glenwood was hurt."

Blaze and Brody locked eyes.

Brody moved to the window again to check on the dogs. "Got any suspects?"

"Maybe. I just want to give you a heads up. Keep your eyes

open around here and call us if there's anything else that happens."

Brody liked Creed immediately. He seemed efficient and smart.

Blaze started pacing the floor. "I wish I had time to get some cameras set up around here before I leave, if you can even buy such a thing in this little town."

"That'd be great," Brody said. "I think I can get Leon to come out and help with that."

Blaze pulled several one hundred dollar bills out of his pocket. "Well, put that on it."

"Thanks. I wonder if Mizz Myrtle would mind having surveillance cameras out there, too," Brody said.

"I think she will be fine with that," said Creed. "I'm going to get back out on the road. Take care, ok? Good to see you again, Blaze."

"You, too."

"I'd better put Chance in the barn and head back to the hospital," Brody said.

Three strong men went out the door, each one determined to make the world around them a better place.

CHAPTER 47

Savannah and Lana sat at a table looking toward the hospital dining room. Lana had been in to visit with Glenwood and he ran them off to go have a decaf latte and some girl time. A couple of men from church had shown up to fill him in on the farm chores they had been doing and to pray over him.

"Daddy's doctor said he would go home tomorrow if he has a good night."

Lana smiled. "That is such good news!"

"I know. His lungs looked inflated in the x ray and he has to come back a few times to check on the wound before the stitches can come out. Considering what he went through, though, it all looks good!" Savannah sipped her coffee and felt thankful deep in her bones.

"So, is Brody out at the farm?"

"Yeah, he's getting some work in and I'm going to text him a grocery list, too. We're not going to need much for a while since people from the church have sent so much food."

"He's a keeper. I thought he would be, remember?" Lana smiled confidently.

"You did. And, you love to be right," Savannah laughed. "We are going to throw a wedding together in just a few weeks. You are going to be busy as my maid of honor, aren't you? I mean, won't you?"

Lana reached out to hug Savannah. "Oh, I would love to! But, are you sure? I mean, why hurry? I always say don't give your power away to a man too quickly."

Savannah understood her best friend's concerns. "I have no doubt. I feel more empowered in this partnership. He is genuine and humble and a man of God. I don't think he will treat me bad later on. I really don't."

"Well, I don't think you are going to get bored with him, so that's good, too."

"Ha! No." Savannah finished her coffee and reached over to shake Lana's coffee cup, to see if it was empty. She took off the white lid and licked the foam off the inside.

"All right. I guess I was finished with that," Lana laughed. "I'll get going. Let me know if you need anything, ok?"

Savannah smiled. "I will, maid of honor to be."

Just then a text came from Brody. It asked if she wanted him to bring her anything when he came back to the hospital in a few hours. He said he had some things to take care of at the farm and for Mizz Myrtle and that Leon would be helping him.

"No. I'm good. You are a good man, Brody! Also, Lana agreed to be my maid of honor," she texted back. "See you in a little while." She ended the text with eight heart emojis, alternating pink and red.

LATER, on the way home from the hospital, Savannah listened to Brody fill her in on the fence lines being cut and the surveillance cameras put up at Mizz Myrtles.

"That is crazy. Nothing like that ever happens around here," she said.

She couldn't help worrying about things. It was how she was wired. No matter how many times, she prayed for God to take away her worry, there always seemed to be something new to worry about. She would have to keep praying on that one for a long time, it seemed.

"Hey, I'm going to run down there and check on her while you take care of the cattle. I want to take her some food, too. The church folks have brought so much, we'll never eat it all."

Brody frowned. "Ok, but remember that Creed said to stay alert. I know you can take care of yourself, but just be careful."

Savannah smiled. "I know. I'll be right back. I'll take my gun. I'll walk through the back fields, and I'll take Cinder."

"Perfect. I'll keep little Chance here with me. Yell if you need me," Brody said.

She knew he had to work hard to trust her and let her go without him. She kissed him longingly to show her appreciation.

IT WAS ALMOST dusk as Savannah neared Mizz Myrtle's acreage. She had enjoyed a quiet walk with Cinder, feeling her long legs stretch into strides that ate up the distance. She had been sitting still so much at the hospital lately, curled up in that stiff recliner beside her daddy's bed.

She didn't let herself think about how bad it would be if she met up with an angry bull on the loose. Those kinds of things were rare. You couldn't get all scared every time something bad happened. You had to keep moving forward. Things were going to be amazing in her future with Brody and her daddy was coming home from the hospital tomorrow.

Cinder suddenly moved in front of her at the exact same time she thought she saw movement just ahead, out of the tree line. He growled a soft low warning sound.

It's a good thing I wasn't singing.

Savannah slowly set the box filled with food containers on the ground and pulled her gun out of her belly band as she cautiously stood up.

Not a bull, at least. A human.

Her gut was firing off alarm bells as she slowly approached the man cutting fence line.

What the heck? Maybe I should stay here in the trees, for cover, and try to take his photo.

She thought that was a great idea, but her feet kept moving her forward. She walked as silently as Cinder did as they approached from the back.

When she got close, she recognized him.

"HOLD IT RIGHT THERE," Savannah kept her gun steady and her eye on his back. "Drop the wire-cutters and turn around. Slowly."

"Don't shoot!" Randy Haner said.

"I'm not going to shoot you," Savannah said.

"Well, I wouldn't feel any guilt about shooting you." Mizz Myrtle was marching across the field from the direction of her house. "In fact, I ought to just shoot you right now. Savannah can call the cops and we'll tell them you attacked us."

Randy Haner looked about ready to throw himself at the little old lady holding a rifle. His eyes jumped from one female to the other, then to the horizon, as if looking for the best way out of the situation that he had made for himself. Wiry energy was rolling off of him in waves that filled Savannah with disgust.

She narrowed her eyes at him as she pulled her phone out of her back pocket and hit the emergency numbers.

"Keep your hands where I can see them. Sit down," she told him.

Mizz Myrtle moved closer. "I've got him, girl. You have them send the cops as fast as they can get out here because I don't have much patience for slimy little men like this!"

Savannah listened to them both as she called for help. She knew Mizz Myrtle was about to preach!

"How could you be so low as to cut my fencing? Why in the world? I've never done anything to you," Mizz Myrtle said.

Randy, sitting on the ground, remained silent, gritting his teeth.

The old woman edged closer and kept him in the rifle's sights. "I mean it, boy. Answer me."

Randy huffed and rolled his eyes. "I wasn't doing anything to you. I don't care about you. I just wanted to give that stuck-up cowboy of hers plenty of work to do. He thinks he is so smart, with Savannah on his arm." He pointed at Savannah.

"Really. Well, did you know my bull got out and gored Savannah's father? He could have died! I hope they throw the book at you. Spoilt rotten piece of no-good excuse for a man!"

Randy looked more worried. "Now, wait a minute. I didn't mean for any of that to happen."

"But here you are, back at it again. Have you even thought about what this will do to your father? Why, he ought to beat you with the biggest Bible in his house until you are crying on the floor."

Randy turned to Savannah. "Hey, this woman is crazy, Savannah. Call my dad. He'll come and get me. There's just been a terrible misunderstanding."

Savannah, finished with the phone call, looked at Randy and wondered what she had ever seen in him. She had to swallow down the urge to shoot him herself. Her voice came out hard and cold. "I am not calling your dad. The cops are coming and I hope it's Creed Ford that they send. And you? You won't be sneaking around causing harm to people and their property again for a long, long time."

"I'm so sorry, honey. I never meant for your dad to get hurt.

He's going to be ok, though, right?" Randy seemed to be reaching around behind his back.

Mizz Myrtle stopped him. "Put your hands on your head, son, before I shoot you."

"She'll do it. Don't be stupid," Savannah said. "And don't call me honey."

She glanced over at Mizz Myrtle who was leaning on a fence post but seemed to be almost enjoying the adventure of it all.

Randy tried to whine about everything again, but Mizz Myrtle shut him down. "There ain't no sense in you even trying to talk to me now. I've got you on camera, on foot, heading over this way. I've got wire-cutters right here at my feet and you didn't even have the sense to put on a pair of gloves, so they have your prints all over them. I'm ashamed of you. Your daddy is a fine preacher and has always tried his best with you."

Savannah couldn't wait to tell Brody about all of this.

"Mizz Myrtle, you are such an amazing woman," she said to her dear old neighbor.

"Well, I'm just taking care of business. That's what good people do. Savannah, surely you can see right here in this moment that all men are different, right?"

"Yes, ma'am, that is the truth!" Savannah laughed. "I have a good one now."

"People get preoccupied while life marches on by. Don't you let your life get away from you, girl. I'm old, and my death is coming. I'm ready to go to Heaven, but I like it here on Earth still. Life is very entertaining." She looked over at Randy and said, "That's why I didn't just go ahead and shoot you. Yet, anyway. I am going to press charges, though, and I bet Glen-wood Stetson will, too."

Savannah picked up the sound of the siren just after Cinder did.

"When they take him away, I'm going to give you a big hug,

and a big box of food I left about twenty yards back," Savannah said.

"Why, thank you, girl. I bet you know someone who will be more than happy to help with my fencing, too." Mizz Myrtle smiled at Savannah and winked.

EPILOGUE

The white and peach flowers on the ends of the pews looked beautiful against the dark wood of the old church. Pleasant Hillside Baptist Church's sanctuary also had matching flowers decorating the large candelabras on either side of the pulpit. The late afternoon sun shone through the colorful stained glass windows.

A hammered dulcimer player was thumping the strings with lively Appalachian songs as the ushers seated the guests.

Blaze Bangfield, with his wide shoulders, escorted his mother down the aisle, while his dad, Scott Bangfield, followed them. He seated them in the front row to the right, as tradition would hold.

The sun slanted across the tops of everyone's head and shoulders as Bobby Joe escorted a woman in a flowing bohemian dress of sage green silk. There was a wreath of flowers sitting atop her long greying hair. He seated her on the front row on the left. Her smile was just like Savannah's.

Skye Stetson looked good for her age. She had flown into the Lexington airport a few days ago and rented a car to drive here for her only daughter's wedding.

The hammered dulcimer stopped playing and the anticipation built.

Malachi Ford, at the front, seated himself on a stool and adjusted his guitar.

Back in the foyer, Savannah smiled at Lana. "Malachi doesn't leave his house for weeks at a time, so I don't know how you talked him into doing music for my wedding, but thanks!"

"Only for you, and maybe for me someday," Lana said. "Besides, as maid-of-honor, I just thought that was part of my job."

"Brody picked the song, and wouldn't tell me what it was going to be. I've been going crazy trying to figure it out." she reached out for Lana's hand.

Savannah was expecting something soft and romantic, so the solid strumming and upbeat tempo surprised her. It only took a few seconds for her to recognize Dierks Bentley's "Woman, Amen." Happy tears started crawling down her face. Could she possibly be any happier?

Lana reached into Glenwood's pocket for his handkerchief and daubed Savannah's tears away as the song rang out over the congregation.

Then a side-door down front opened and the pastor came out followed by Brody and Bobby Joe, looking handsome in their dark jeans and cowboy boots with turquoise plaid shirts and a peach colored rose boutonnieres.

The organist began to play Pachelbel's Canon in D and everyone looked back to watch.

Lana Ford, the maid of honor, walked slowly down the aisle. She wore a peach and white floral chiffon dress, longer in the back, so that her beautiful cowboy boots could be seen. Her long hair was up in intricate loose braids around her head. She carried a bouquet of peach roses and white peonies. She only had eyes for Bobby Joe, standing beside Brody as she made her way to her spot.

The organ music swelled as Savannah came into view at the back, on the arm of Glenwood Stetson. The congregation stood up. Many people looked at them and had tears in their eyes, as they thought about what a miracle it was that Glenwood was walking his daughter down the aisle after his close call.

Glenwood used a cane and they went very slowly.

Savannah was every inch a blushing bride in her rustic lace wedding dress. The tan and white cowboy boots received the attention they deserved, framed in the high-low hem of the dress.

Her hair was fashioned in a whimsical side-swept braid so that the back of the dress could be seen. Tiny peach and white flowers were woven into her hair and loose strands framed her face.

Tears came to her eyes as she looked at Brody standing at the front of the church, looking so handsome and strong.

How my life has changed! God in Heaven, thank you for this opportunity to make a life together with my Brody. Help me to be a good partner to him all of my days on this earth.

It seemed as if that walk down the aisle was in slow motion.

And thank you, Lord, that daddy is walking me down the aisle. Give him strength. Oh, and thanks for mom being here, too.

"Who gives this bride to the groom in marriage?" the pastor asked.

"Her mother and I do," said Glenwood.

Beulah Burton cleared her throat loudly enough for people to notice. Annabelle patted her back.

Savannah's father kissed her on the cheek and then turned to sit beside his ex-wife, Skye.

Savannah handed off her beautiful bouquet of pale peach roses and white peonies to Lana. They exchanged smiles while Lana nodded encouragingly.

Savannah turned toward Brody as he took both her hands in

his. She noticed there were tears in his eyes also. She felt like she was visibly trembling with nervous happiness.

Malachi Ford and a teenage girl named Trisha, who often did solos with the choir, stepped up to the microphone as a music track began playing the duet version of the Shania Twain song "From This Moment On."

The audience smiled as they enjoyed the words and harmonies soaring to the rafters in the old church. When the key change hit the high point of the song, Savannah wondered if the guests got shivers up the back of their necks like she did.

It was the perfect song choice for the happiness of this day.

Savannah trembled as the words to the song were whispered here and there by Brody, whose look was so intense it made her wonder how she deserved to be this happy.

"I will love you," Brody whispered during the chorus.

"I promise you this," Savannah whispered back. She realized she had made the perfect song choice, too.

"A Kentucky Cowboy's love," whispered Brody.

The pastor's baritone voice rang out over everyone.

"Savannah Kaye Stetson and Brody Boone Bangfield, today you are surrounded by your friends and family, all of whom have gathered here to witness your marriage and to share in the joy of this special occasion.

Today as you join yourselves together there is a vast and unknown future stretching out before you. The possibilities and potentials of your married life are great. The task of choosing your values and making real your dreams falls upon your shoulders.

Through your commitment to each other, may you grow and nurture a love that makes both of you better people, a love that continues to give you great joy, and also a passion for living that provides you both with energy and patience to face all the responsibilities of life."

Savannah almost laughed when she realized she didn't know

Brody's middle name until their wedding day. BBB. She would tease him about those initials later, but for now it was time for her vows.

Her voice was stronger than she thought it might be as she laid her heart open for Brody in front of everyone here. "Brody Boone Bangfield, my Kentucky cowboy, I, Savannah Kaye Stetson, promise to always be there for you, to shelter and hold your love as the most precious gift in my life. I will be truthful and honor you. You and Jesus are the most important parts of my life. I will care for you always and stand by you in times of sorrow and joy, forever nurturing the love I feel for you."

It thrilled her to the core to hear Brody say the words to her.

"Savannah Kaye Stetson, oh... I, Brody Boone Bangfield," he said and then swallowed loudly.

"BBB," she said softly and winked.

He smiled and went on. "I promise to always be there for you, to shelter and hold your love as the most precious gift in my life. I will be truthful and honor you. You and God are the most important parts of my life. I will care for you always and stand by you in times of sorrow and joy, forever nurturing the love I feel for you."

After the exchange of rings, Savannah took her flowers back from Lana. She turned toward the congregation, holding her husband's hand.

She noticed her father reach out and squeeze Skye's hand and give her his handkerchief as she smiled through her happy tears. Savannah appreciated them both being here for her, and sitting together. She hoped that handkerchief wasn't too damp already.

"And now, by the power vested in me by the Commonwealth of Kentucky, I hereby pronounce you husband and wife. You may kiss your bride."

Savannah promised as much as she could to Brody in that kiss. She had to remember that she was in church and many people were watching because she did not want the kiss to end. Its intensity was something she knew she would always remember.

The organ music swelled with Mozart's "Organ Fantasie in F" k594. Savannah had taken the organist's advice on this music choice and she was glad she had as she and Brody walked down the aisle together, followed by Lana and Bobby Joe.

Without a pause the music went into the overture to The Marriage of Figaro as the family was escorted out of the church. The organist played until all the congregation was dismissed, row by row.

The organist made the old instrument sing with happiness that matched Brody and Savannah as they exited Pleasant Hillside Baptist Church and stepped, together, into the sunshine of their future in Bourbon Creek, Kentucky.

THE END

IF YOU ENJOYED THIS BOOK, I sure would appreciate if you would leave me a review. It helps more than you know.

Join the Facebook Group Bourbon Creek Romance so you won't miss new releases in the series.

There's a free cookbook download in the works that will have favorite recipes from the characters.

My website is dinahpike.com but I don't have much there yet - the characters of Bourbon Creek Romance 2 want me to write their story first!

ACKNOWLEDGMENTS

Special thanks to:

Sarra Cannon, of Heart Breathings, HB90 Bootcamp, and the Publish and Thrive course

Jessica Sasser, alpha reader, and betas: Mom, Cindy Sullivan, Jenny Miller, and Lynn Nelson

Marsha Blankenship, for everything to do with cowboy boots, guns, belly bands, and trucks

Sahvannah Marie McDowell, for horse knowledge

Monte Ward, for bourbon knowledge

Dr Frank Shuler, for trama surgeon insights

Emily Jamison and Tim Holmes, local musician/songwriters

Jesse Thomas guitars

ABOUT THE AUTHOR

Dinah Pike is a retired National Board Certified teacher of gifted students. She writes small-town romance, musicals, and children's picture books. She loves her family, cooking, Crossfit Countdown, Kentucky, and dogs.

This is Dinah's first romance novel.

28989941R00128